The Lesser Madonnas

The Lesser Madonnas

Stories

A. Rooney

MADVILLE
PUBLISHING

LAKE DALLAS, TEXAS

FIRST EDITION

This is a work of fiction, and is not intended to resemble anyone
living or dead.

ACKNOWLEDGMENTS

"Shelly and the Slipping Away" received an Honorable Mention in
Glimmer Train's 2014 Family Matters Fiction Contest.

Requests for permission to reprint or reuse material
from this work should be sent to:

Permissions
Madville Publishing
PO Box 358
Lake Dallas, TX 75065

Cover design: Kim and Jacqueline Davis
Author photo: Jacqueline Davis

ISBN: 978-1-956440-87-4 paperback
978-1-956440-88-1 ebook

Library of Congress Control Number: 2023952549

Table of Contents

*Men and teeth. I had a hard time keeping both
when I was alive.*

—"Shelley and the Slipping Away"

Shelley and
the Slipping Away

The whole time I was a teenager I had the dream of losing my teeth. And a different way every time. But not all of them, just the incisors. In a car accident. One of the tough girls in school. My brothers.

Then the first one did come out. Makes it sound like kindergarten and your first tooth, it came out. I was at a party in college. My date and I went upstairs to roll around. We were drunk and trying to get his pants off without taking his shoes off. He was all over the place with his elbows. Cut my lip and I felt the tooth stuck in my throat. Got up and went to look in the bathroom mirror. He was upset that we weren't going to have sex, so I apologized.

Men and teeth. I had a hard time keeping both when I was alive.

But looking back I realize, with teeth you could go anywhere, do anything. Without them you just kind of disappeared in people's minds. They looked away. And that's when the disappearing really began for me.

In my family I was the one who got called the others' names: Margress, *no, ah,* Shelley. Kathreen, *no, ah, let's see,* Shelley. Five of us. Not a big, big deal. It happens in families with a forgetful father, and you're the fifth.

There I am, though, I see myself. Lining up with this one and that one, putting my hand over my mouth, not speaking, not finishing things. College, a bicycle ride, my dinner with a date.

1.

See the little girl with crayons at the table, handling them delicately, putting them back in the box tips up. Jazzberry and Goldenrod, Purple Heart, Timberwolf, Red Orange. Scribbling away even as she gets older. Crayons her best friends.

Whenever things happened in the motels, when my father would drink and mother would shriek, I'd find leftover paper, cardboard that was thrown away, old envelopes, the side of the dryer once. I loved to draw and I had a family. Not my own family, but the one I created. There was the good father and mother who worked and didn't have to move all the time, a nice dog who came when he was called, and their only child, a daughter, Mahogany. In my drawings the girl was always being asked to do a chore, and she was the champion of chores: Coffee for mother at the market, yard jobs for father outside. A wide-eyed girl in the images, she always felt like a princess for having done the chores, and like she had meaning to the father and mother. Some of the pictures had captions, but not all.

I started off with stick figures and gradually they got bigger and better and had more things going on. They looked a little like Sister Gertrude's drawings, the crayon ones, only maybe not as detailed. She was my hero and I tried to make my pictures look like hers. There was a photo of me from grade school, concentrating very hard, with a crayon sticking up out of each hand. I had boxes full of them at the end and didn't know what to do with them. And all kinds of little notebooks.

Which is why I liked Motherwell's paintings: crayon blobs and crosses, no people or places.

There were others but the first place I remember really well was a motel between Monte Vista and Del Norte. Ten units. White with bright green trim. A big advertising sign on the end for something. Let me think. Walter's Beer, from Pueblo.

The people that owned it had died and the children moved to Las Cruces. We were there from kindergarten to the end of third grade. My father did everything: maintenance, front desk, housekeeping. My mother worked in town at different places. Every time it was my father struggling to keep it together, then losing it. Keeping it together, then losing it. He lost it in the bank and the next day we were on our way to Colorado Springs.

And there I am, being left outside Walsenburg, at a rest stop, before I-25 when it was still a two-lane—'85-87. My father had finished most of a six pack, it was a big station wagon, he could easily have missed me, but I was there until way after dark. Good thing it was late spring. He was upset and, of course, I apologized.

In the car I colored in my notebook—busy, busy, frightened. A big wide border of Black, my imaginary family in Yellow Orange, the dog Sepia. Till we were there at the new motel on Nevada Avenue, page after page, I couldn't stop. I knew what would happen if I began to cry.

After that was where the listening started.

It originated with my brothers. The girls, the three of us, stayed in a room with my parents, but the boys lived in the rooms that were vacant, moving from day to day. At the door vent I could hear them talking about running away, how they'd seen up a girl's skirt, how they hated a certain teacher, running backs and quarterbacks, and what they wanted to do when they got older.

Then I got braver and started listening at the doors of different guests. I liked it when men and women would say oh, oh, oh after the lights were out and they'd gotten quiet. But I didn't like it when they hurt each other. The men mostly doing the hurting.

I listened when they were drunk and followed them to their rooms, hearing them talk to no one, arguing, falling, spilling their change in the hallway, cursing the TV.

Once, while I was listening at the vent, a tipsy man, very fat, came to the door suddenly in enormous boxers and dragged me into his room by the arm. My brothers heard the screams and saved me.

I liked the night my parents agreed to have another brother, they knew it would be a boy, and I heard them talking about what to call him. Their lips touching, I could hear that, and when it got very quiet, their breathing together.

When they began to argue so much I pressed my ear to the door and heard them say my name. I fell asleep listening so hard and woke up in my own bed.

The night my father made the decision to go away for a job, to stop doing motel work, to leave us in Denver, I heard that, too, and knew before my brothers and sisters. When the money didn't come we all heard my grandparents say they were sending my uncle to live with us. For a time there I lost the ability to hear.

But the crayons were always my friends, with drawings plus a note and a date at the top.

2.

I'd seen him going and coming through a little basement door, down five steps with a handrail. He'd walk up to Colorado

Boulevard and meet other old men at a breakfast place and then stop at the bar after. When he got home, whatever shape he was in, he would work on his truck.

This was one of those nice old green pick-ups that was in good shape, but not restored. I helped out at the motel some days when the Indian people needed to do something or wanted off. The old man was too old to drive and he would walk slowly, slowly past and not look up. It was parked up in the backyard of the house under a tarp.

There were people who lived upstairs, but it seemed they barely knew he was there. Then a gap of a few days went by and no old man, or at least not when I was at the motel. On a break I walked by the house and he was lying in the basement stairwell, one arm reaching up. He'd slipped and fallen and was dead. No one had seen him but me.

When I knocked on the door upstairs they didn't answer. And when I called the police and the ambulance came, they got his information out of his wallet, put him on a gurney and drove away.

I went through his things, including the glove compartment, and tried to find contact information, even friends, but he didn't have anything in the apartment except another change of clothes and cans of soup in the cabinet. His sheets were gray and the covers were in tatters.

The extra key to the truck was on a nail inside the door, the original probably in the pants he was wearing. When I wanted a ride home after work one day, I got the key and tried it in the ignition. It turned over once and then started right up. I expected the people upstairs to come running out.

Because it was close to the motel, some nights when I worked late I slept in the little apartment and fell asleep to the sound of scurrying. When my lease was up I moved the few things I had over. No one had seen me or said anything to me.

Sometimes I could hear the soft shuffling of slippers on the floor upstairs.

He was an old man who nobody ever came looking for—nobody that I could see. And as time went on, and his mail piled up, I opened it. I paid his fees on the license plates and put his Social Security checks in the drawer. When I knocked the second time to ask about the rent, they didn't open the door then either.

About the old man and his life, I never learned much. He had a checking account with a few thousand dollars in it, credit cards with no balances, a dentist who insisted he come for his next laser treatment, and a doctor who reminded him it was time for his bi-annual prostate exam. There was no TV and no phone, and all the light bulbs were burned out. A toilet and sink, both stained, were tucked away on the far side of the main room.

In my sleep I could see the old man, what I remembered of him, in apparitions. He was slightly hunched and wore a billed cap with ear flaps. One eye was bigger than the other and had milky circles, like an agate. In the other room—there were just the two rooms—I could always hear him making soup.

During the day I would sit in his shifty chair and draw dark scenes with my crayons. For a few hours, when the sun was in position and the drape was back, the light would move through the apartment's single window like a lighthouse beam, as though it were searching for him.

Winter light was much different than summer.

I'd never drawn geometrical shapes before; it had mostly been free form kinds of scenes with people in them, often in front of what might pass for a motel. But in the little apartment I began scratching out angles—the frame of the door, the wood and concrete support beams and posts, the chair, the window. And I drew the shafts of the streaming light.

Then one night a figure came into the room, a shape. I couldn't see his face. Wilson, he said, it's me, Roland. And then Roland sat in the chair taking his shoes off, his shirt and pants. I could hear him, not see him in the dark basement, and I was terrified.

Roland said he'd been away working the oil fields in Canada, and there was a vague scent of petroleum. At every moment I was prepared to sit up and say I'm not Wilson, I'm Shelley, but I waited.

Roland approached the bed and he was naked, a naked Black man with an erection, I could see him as he got closer, and he drew the covers back and slid in next to me. You asleep Wilson, or you dead? Roland asked. You don't smell dead. And he put his hands on my backside and then my stomach, finally my crotch, his hand searching for the graspable, missing something.

"Wilson," he said sitting up, "you ain't Wilson," and he put one hand around my throat, squeezed it, and lifted me. "What you done with Wilson? Where Wilson?"

I was choking and couldn't talk, and what would I have said if I could? That I'd found Wilson dead, that I'd taken over his apartment, been driving his truck, and that in some ways I'd become Wilson?

Roland slapped my face hard and continued to say "Where Wilson? Where Wilson?" as he backed away and hurriedly put on his clothes in the dark. I still couldn't speak, though I tried to say something, that I was sorry, that yes Wilson was dead. It was only after he'd gone, after I'd recovered my voice, after I'd run my tongue around my mouth, that I could taste the blood and found another tooth missing, this one perched between my cheek and gum.

I stayed in the apartment for a few years and bought a lock for the door. But Roland never came again, though I was terrified he might.

Before all this happened—Wilson, working at the motel—I was kind of married, we'd lived together for eleven years,

Randy and me. I worked at a small natural foods store; he was with the city, in the pools division. It was older hippies at the store and they didn't have any problem with a gal who was missing teeth. Only two then.

You wanna? That's how Randy approached it, us living together. Yeah, I said, I guess, sure. His sister had an Airstream they'd taken the wheels off and we lived there for a while. We'd started sitting together on my break, eating stew and oyster crackers from the deli bar.

My family stopped including me in things because they didn't like Randy. They said he wasn't very smart and he cursed too much. Which is true, on both counts. He also peed on the floor next to the toilet, ate with his mouth open, used my towel to wipe his dirty hands, never washed a dish, and wore the same underwear for days. But he was okay. At least he was somebody.

I'm going, I said one day to Randy. This was when I realized he wasn't somebody enough and I didn't want to spend any more time with him.

"Sit down," he said.

"I'm going. I need to go."

He stood in front of the door.

I sat on the sofa.

"Let's go in the bedroom."

That was another thing. He wasn't so good in there.

"No," I said. "I can't."

I lost number three when Randy tried to kiss me, and when I resisted, he head-butted me instead.

I started renting a room at the motel by the week and Nisha gave me a special price. Half the place was rented by the week. I was still a checker at the market, but that's when the economy took a dive and they had to send people home. They gave me a few hours, but less than half time.

Madam Ada was there then, the fortune teller, who told people everything was auspicious. When we weren't busy at the front desk and it was late, I'd visit Madam, but leave the door open to see the office. She was from India, too, but not the same town as Nisha. And when no one was around and the door was open, I could hear her cursing, saying shitdamnit with her lilting accent.

Really, I said to her one night, really, when she'd told me everything was auspicious.

"You are wanting to really know?" she asked.

"Yes," and I was thinking at the time, *God, what else could happen*, and that Madam was a fake.

But she said there was more on the way—that things were going to get worse before they got better. And then she added that the number four looked auspicious. That was four months before Roland relieved me of my fourth tooth.

I asked her a few times if she ever read her own fortune and she would only shake her head and say, "It has been foretold."

While I'd been at the motel, a number of gals had come and gone, renters. Some with men friends, some by themselves. And all of them hard to get to know. With that faraway look in their eyes. Which was probably what they thought when they looked at me.

And during that time the old beautician next door passed. Somebody discovered her in her house dead of an overdose of pain pills. She had the kind of skin cancer that kills you. I'd gotten to know her a little. She cut and styled my hair for free when I needed it for an interview. She even invited me to her house, but I never went.

Nobody rented the shop after she was gone and whenever I got the chance, in the evening light or first thing, with my crayons I sketched out an imaginary Aleen looking out the front window, then Madam Ada reading palms in her room, Nisha and her husband standing in front of the Bel-Care sign, and a couple of the unfortunate women leaning against their doors.

I did go to Aleen's funeral, though, and it was a little odd. Mostly very old women with big hair who still made themselves up every day. Her former business partner was there, Deeda, living in Palm Springs, but nobody in her family. I usually went to those events and avoided eye contact, hand over mouth, wrapped things up in napkins, and slipped out without anyone noticing. But this one didn't have anything to wrap up.

Aleen changed me to a shorty. My whole life I'd had long hair and always had a hard time taking care of it, full of rats and long, uneven bangs. But one day she talked me into cutting it. She just said it was time, and it probably was. My scalp was always so sensitive, I wouldn't let anyone touch it and I didn't like washing or brushing my hair. But she had a way, I don't know, of doing it.

"You have a head," she told me once when she was massaging it, and at the time I knew what that meant. She sat in the chair next to me that day and said she never liked hair that much, but it was something to do for a girl from Alamosa. Fifty years of doing something you didn't like, but that you were pretty good at.

3.

The walk looked familiar, but I couldn't place it right away. Head down, arms swinging just a quarter swing. And he stopped to look at the truck, put both hands on it, reached inside the cab. But let me back up first and say I was there in the office because Nisha had gone home for four weeks. It was spring and she hadn't been to India for a while.

Rajiv, her husband, stayed and made a pest of himself. He

wasn't that good with the office or guests, and he did a bad job with the rooms. Whatever he did I had to do over. And then there was the touching. First it was a hand on my shoulder when I was signing someone in. Then around the waist with a little touch of my boob. In the room vacuuming or tucking in the sheets, I had to push him away when he approached me from the back.

Nisha took all day and showed me the books and the checks before she left, but I'd already been doing them part-time. I missed Nisha a lot after the first day she was gone. It didn't take long before I realized Rajiv had been double-writing checks to the linen supplier, for instance, or to the people who restriped the parking lot, and then cashing the checks when they sent the overage back. Who knows what he was doing with the money, but I can only imagine. And stealing from his own wife?

Plus, while Nisha was away, Rajiv brought these shady characters around and he took money out of the register.

"Edgar Wilson, Jr.," he said when he stood at the counter, "and that's my grandfather's truck."

"He gave it to me," I said.

"That's a lie," Edgar said. "He would never give that truck to anyone. He bought it new in 1950 and had it his whole life."

"Your grandfather died," I said. "He slipped and fell on the steps and no one found him."

"Who's there in his apartment, the door's locked?"

"Me."

"So you got his truck and his place too?"

"Yeah, and I'm sleeping in his same bed. Nothing's changed."

"I came here for one reason," Edgar said.

"No problem," I said. "Here's the keys."

"It wasn't to get the truck. Better that you have it and are getting some use from it."

"Then why are you here? To visit?"

"I came here to kill my grandfather."

He shifted a pistol from his back pocket to his front so I could see it.

"After your grandfather died, Roland stopped by one night, but he didn't stay."

"I'm surprised he didn't try something."

"He did but he was looking for somebody else."

"Somebody like me probably. I'd kill Roland if I ever saw him."

Edgar and I talked for a time and then he left abruptly before I closed everything up.

Rajiv was there overnight and I went back to the little apartment. I'd made soup and was eating it and reading the newspaper in bed when Edgar knocked. It was about one.

"Would it be all right," he said, "if I stayed here, like off in a corner?"

He had his sleeping bag, a pad and a pillow.

"Yeah, I guess so, long as you don't make any trouble."

I pointed to the front room and Edgar threw his things down.

"I haven't quite gotten rid of all the critters," I said. "So you might have some visitors when we turn the lights out."

Edgar used the toilet loudly, then stripped to his loose undershorts and got in the bag. He had the same build as his grandfather, small and rangy, with hit-and-miss whiskers and hair that had been matted down with a cap. I listened to his breathing and it never seemed to settle into sleep.

More than once I turned and turned again and in the middle of the night Edgar came and stood by my bed.

"If you wouldn't mind," he said pausing, "if it would be okay. I have a hard time sleeping alone." He was shivering even though the apartment was warm and he'd been in a thick bag.

My first thought was to tell him to go back to bed, but I drew the covers back and he got in.

He kept his hands to himself but snuggled up to my back.

"Don't worry," Edgar said, "I'm in between."

I turned and faced him and gently put my hand on his arm.

"What's in between, Edgar?" I said.

"I have been with men but don't like it," he said. "And don't know how to be with women."

"What happened, Edgar? Did something happen with your grandfather and Roland?"

"Ah, we were driving in the green truck to take Roland back to his job. He was working at the sawmill in Libby, in Montana, up near the border. We stopped for the night at a motel. There was only one bed. Roland put blankets on the floor and I slept with my grandfather. That night, that was the night he came and got in bed with us and then he went at me."

"Did your grandfather try and stop him or do anything?"

"He never said one word, even after I was crying and begging for his help."

He waited a long time to continue.

"I'm sorry Edgar," I said. "I'm sorry."

Edgar put his arms around me and held me tight. We were still face to face and he tried hard not to tear up. He stopped shivering when I put my arms around him. Before long, his breathing deepened, and he fell off into a heavy, spastic sleep.

In the morning I tried to move his arms, but they were locked around me. I looked at his boyish face and kissed him on the cheeks and lips. Within a few moments he woke and was startled to see me there. He released his arms and neither of us spoke.

While we lay there Edgar became erect and I put him inside me. I kissed him again and without moving he climaxed.

"Why you got all these boxes of crayons around here?" Edgar said when he got up and made us some soup and eggs.

I showed him the notebooks and he saw the room and the sun and the different ways I'd drawn them. He flipped through some of the collections in the crate next to the bed.

"How long?" Edgar asked, touching one of them.

"Since I was a little girl," I said.

"These are nice, I like them," he said. "How come you let me stay here? How come you let me sleep with you?"

"Oh, maybe, I don't know. Maybe I thought you needed it. And it's been a while since I had anybody in my bed, except Roland, and I don't think that counts."

I asked him about the gun, said I was worried he might get up in the middle of the night and use it on me. He went and got it and showed me it didn't have any bullets.

"Would you have killed your grandfather if he'd have been here instead of me?"

"I'd probably killed myself before I'd killed him, but I would've made him answer some questions."

"Have you thought about killing yourself, Edgar?"

"Plenty of times. Especially right after."

"What did you do when you saw your grandfather again?"

"I never saw him. If I knew he was coming to the house I made it a point to be away."

"What are you going to do today? I have to work this morning and then I was thinking about taking a drive in the mountains this afternoon, it's been so nice and the snow is mostly off the roads."

I told him which of the canyons I was going to drive up and invited him to join me.

He said he thought he'd better get back on the road. That there was a spring storm headed for eastern Colorado and he wanted to see if he couldn't get ahead of it. I asked if I could give him the sandbags in the back of the truck, to help with traction if he got into snow. We pulled them off and threw them in his trunk.

"Gift of your grandfather," I said. "They were already in the truck when I started driving it."

"It'll probably turn out that I'll need them and will thank him, that fucking old bastard."

Edgar looked at my missing teeth and asked what happened. I told him there was a different story for each one, none very interesting.

He stood looking at me with his arms at his side as I was gathering myself to go.

"Goodbye, Edgar," I said and kissed him on the cheek. "Lock it and pull the door shut when you leave."

When I got to the Bel-Care just before eight, Rajiv was at the desk tapping his pen. Nothing had happened through the night, but he was ready to go. Before he left he gave me the report about who was staying and who was leaving, and then patted me on the backside. He also told me if I had a few minutes to put the cans of paint behind the counter in the vacant rooms.

"Shouldn't we wait for Nisha on the paint?"

He said it would look good to her when she got back.

Within a few minutes, Edgar was there with coffee.

"Just thought I'd say thanks, you know, for, em, for last night, I...," and his chest began to heave and then tears came on and with his hands he tried to say something else, like he'd spent years working at not crying, that he'd felt stuck in a bed between Roland and his grandfather, and that he was looking forward to relief and the possibility of getting on with his life.

But he couldn't say that, and he touched me on the hand and then was out the door and in his car.

As soon as Rajiv appeared I maneuvered around him

and went to clean rooms. Just after noon, having done the least acceptable job of housekeeping, I got in the truck and was gone.

People say your life passes in front of you when you die, but it was the windshield and doors and bed of the truck that passed in front of me, again and again, and then I was out the driver's door when the belt came loose and the white of the ground, the green-brown of the pines, and the cloudy sky joined the floating mix, like one of my crayon drawings.

And a final tooth.

I could've taken a number of routes, Lefthand Canyon, Golden Gate Canyon, Eldorado Canyon, but I chose Coal Creek Canyon, one I really liked, and I was going to stop in Nederland for something to eat.

The road was still snow packed where the sun had not penetrated, and I could feel the tail give way on the turns. Halfway up it began to snow lightly and the truck spun around and came to rest against the guard rail. I got out and walked up the road, shook my hands loose, and looked for something to throw in the back, but everything was too heavy. *Maybe if I drove slowly the truck would be all right,* I thought then. And it worked.

Until it didn't.

There near the top of the canyon. I figured we were done. But over the side it went. No steering. The engine revving loud. The nose hitting trees. The roof crushing. Bouncing like nothing. Finally wedging to a stop.

But I was gone and out by then. On one of the tumbles. Quickly, painlessly over as soon as I struck something.

Then the wait.

The first night.

The second.

And Edgar. Having come back because of the snow on 70. One pass. Two, three, four.

His little car slipping as well.
But finally, him crawling down the ravine.
At the truck first.
And after searching, me.
Kneeling in the snow.
Wailing.
Then loading the pistol.
A first shot, another, another, another.
Into the truck.
And a fifth.

Reena in Decline

This was what you would see if you drove by her stop in the morning and Reena was there: a once-attractive woman, compact, hair pulled back, talking and gesturing to anyone listening. But she might be especially animated if she discovered the person she was talking to had had their license taken away or couldn't afford a car or was just down on their luck.

When she boarded her bus, she often said more than greetings to drivers, things like "Ten and two, sir," and "Mitts on the frozen rope," in reference to the position of his hands and handling the steering wheel safely.

At her office building she reminded the smokers they needed to be at least ten feet away from the door, even if it was snowing, and then she became dramatic about coughing as she moved through the crowd.

Inside, Reena had somehow managed to get herself next to a window and as a marketing assistant, according to corporate protocol, that was unacceptable. But she remained there because the administration was never sure what to do about it, and Reena made it difficult.

The company was an engineering firm in southeast Denver, mostly men, that specialized in wastewater treatment plants. Reena's job was to draft materials that told people how important it was to have wastewater treated and how happy they would be once it was. These materials, of course, would always be reviewed by a number of layers above her. The reviewers, at least at the first level, knew to be on the lookout for "Reenaisms," statements like "What's not to love about treated wastewater?" or "Imagine yourself in a village with all that bad water piling up," or "Think of it as a basic right for citizens of the planet, like food and water and TV."

These were not incendiary statements, but her writing was, at times, marginal and required line editing for tenses and misspellings, something engineers, even literate ones, were not accustomed to doing. But Reena saw herself as a grammarian and content expert and she almost never accepted changes without an argument.

Most days Reena brought her lunch, which was generally half of whatever she'd made for dinner the night before. But because she was in the marketing department, through some logic, she made it part of her duty to order breakfasts or lunches for company meetings and then take home whatever was left.

She liked to say "It's company policy not to allow it" whenever a department asked if they could keep the food from their meeting. So Reena would cover the bagels or cold cuts or fruit with plastic and whisk the tray away to her office, later to be carried like a trophy on the bus to her condominium.

Because she thought she was poorly paid, Reena also reasoned that packages of coffee from the break room, printer paper, cleaning supplies, and toilet tissue were an entitlement and there for the taking. Fellow employees knew that she stuffed them in her always-full backpack, but because they occasionally filched things themselves, nothing was ever said.

BALANCE: $35,490

Every day of the last week of January, as the engineering company assessed how much money it was making and how much work it appeared they had, Human Resources began sending people home. When the staff gathered in small groups to gossip about their chances of being sacked and who had recently been sent home, Reena stayed at her desk and told people she was too busy to talk and too valuable to be fired.

On Friday of that week, after Reena had wrapped a breakfast tray up, the woman who sat next to her was called into the vice president's office. She returned in tears and began gathering her photographs and plants. Reena said goodbye and helped her pack her things in a box, but more than anything she felt relief that the storm had seemingly passed over her desk and landed on her neighbor's. After the woman left, she thought she could have been more helpful early on by telling her not to take so many coffee breaks.

In the afternoon, the manager came into her office and asked how she was feeling.

"Fine," Reena told her, "how should I be feeling?"

The manager almost looked surprised to see her there.

A few minutes later, the vice president's assistant called and invited her to come upstairs for a meeting.

Because it was Friday afternoon, she thought she was going to be given an award of some kind, possibly a promotion.

Mr. Furman had been with the Environmental Protection Agency before he went to work for the engineering company. Reena had always felt a kinship with him, even an attraction, and she especially liked his mustache, though there were a few times when she thought it needed trimming.

Mr. Furman's assistant offered Reena bottled water while she waited. But she declined because when she was even the slightest bit nervous, like she was that day, and drank water, it almost invariably made her want to pee.

On the assistant's back table was what looked like a plaque in a manila envelope, and Reena was certain she was going to receive an award.

"Oh, yes, Reena," Mr. Furman said when he opened his door. "Thank you for stopping by. Please come in. May I get you a bottle of water?"

Reena said no, thank you, and crossed her legs. That was the first time she'd ever been inside his office and on his walls were photos of himself at wastewater treatment plants in Saudi Arabia, Ecuador, and one of the Northwest Territories, with Inuits.

"Reena," Mr. Furman began, "is it alright if I call you just Reena?"

"Sure, or you can call me Reen, Mr. Furman. It's my family nickname."

Reena cleared her throat and spoke before he could continue.

"In advance of getting the award, Mr. Furman, I'd like to make a suggestion. Why not begin calling the recycled water that comes from wastewater treatment plants victory water? Kind of a take-off on victory gardens, if you remember those."

"That's a great idea, Reena. But the real reason I called you up here today is because the company has had three bad quarters, as you no doubt have heard, and we need to make some personnel changes. Do you understand what I mean?"

"Downsizing a few people, yeah? Well, and I couldn't agree more with the choices the company has made so far. The woman you sent home from my department, the one who used to sit next to me, Terri, she spent too much time with online catalogs and took way too many breaks. But if the company asks, if you ask Mr. Furman, I'll gladly pick up her assignments."

She smiled at the vice president like they were old friends.

Reena was poised to say something else, something about the new brand of coffee in the break room, when Mr. Furman held up his hand.

"I asked you up here to my office because today, unfortunately, is your last day at this company, Reena. We're sending you home. I hate to see you go because you've been such a valuable addition to the Marketing Department and you always have such good ideas."

"Wait, what did you just say?" She had been concentrating on his mustache.

"I'm sorry, Reena, but we're going to have to let you go. This is your final day. In fact, someone will be here to help you get your things together and then escort you out. It doesn't reflect on your personality. It's simply a fiscal adjustment that's necessary for the life of the company."

"No."

"What's that?"

"I said no, you can't fire me. I'm too valuable to this company."

"You are a valuable member of the marketing team, Reena, but we've got to make some across-the-board cuts in order to address potential income shortfalls."

Reena stood and told Mr. Furman he should think about it over the weekend. She was sure by Monday he would change his mind. She wasn't sure, though, that she would make it to the ladies' room without having an accident.

Security was there waiting in the exterior office when Reena walked out. To Mr. Furman's assistant she said, "Tell your boss that's an awful-looking mustache he's wearing."

BALANCE: $139.54

The garden-level condo Reena lived in was located equidistant from The Shotgun Men's Club and Hooters. Sometimes when she rode the bus she could tell the person sitting next to her was a dancer and she would often say to them how nice their make-up or clothing looked.

On the Friday she was fired from the engineering company, Reena carried a tray of breakfast and lunch items on the bus and as the thoughts of the day circled around her, she felt like dumping them out the window. At her stop, men who had just come from Hooters, who'd been drinking, tried to take the tray away from her. With three of them it didn't take much and when they laughed she flipped them off and told them to keep the damn thing, she didn't want it anyway. They pursued her and said they were only kidding, they were sorry, and she hurried on to the bank to see how much money she had in her account.

In the last month she'd had to take her cat to the veterinarian twice: once when she found a cyst on its hip and they had to remove it, and another time when it continued to have diarrhea everywhere but inside the litter box. The bill came to just over a thousand dollars. She also had fallen behind on her homeowner's association dues and was only able to pay half, three months, and they said because it was a repeat they would have to begin foreclosure proceedings. The remaining HOA fees came to $600. The fact was, she had never been very good at saving money.

Reena stood holding her receipt showing how much she had in her account: a little more than $138. She wanted to eat noodles at Meikong Pho, two blocks away, after she'd had a chance to clean up and feed the cat. Then she wanted to try and catch an early movie. Her car was out of gas, though, so she was either going to have to walk or take the bus over the interstate to the theater.

At the restaurant, Nguyen, the owner, came and sat with her and they talked about his family and what she wanted for dinner. She liked the Special Bowl, #54, and he said he would make it just for her. She tried to tell him that only a few hours earlier she'd been fired from her job, but because his English was not that good, he told her congratulations and shook her hand, then went to the kitchen to make her order. Reena called him back and suggested he not put so much lettuce and bean sprouts in the bottom.

After dinner, looking very apologetic, Nguyen brought her credit card back when she paid and told her "Not work, very sorry, maybe machine." Reena only had one credit card and no debit account and when she looked distressed, he said, "You pay later, you good customer, no problem."

Reena thought that she might have over spent her limit on the card and that the company cut her off. She would just have to go back to the ATM at the bank and pull thirty or forty dollars out, if there was still money in it by the time she got there.

The movie was about a horse who'd been conscripted into the military during World War I. It initially was in service to the British, then was captured by the Germans. It had an enormous will to live and was involved in a number of harrowing experiences, including being tangled up in barbed wire in the middle of a battlefield.

Reena was not a horse person herself, she'd only owned cats, but she identified with the beautiful animal and wept most of the way through the movie. She stopped crying when she discovered Mr. Furman and his wife down the aisle and across from her.

In the closing moments of the film, she developed a list of things she was going to say to him, despite the presence of his wife. During the movie she could see them holding hands and looking at each other lovingly, and both wearing nice clothes. She wanted to go over and rip Mr. Furman's mustache off.

When it had ended, Reena stood quickly and approached the man, bent on giving him a real piece of her mind. But when she got close, she could see it was someone else, someone who didn't even have a mustache, and she was upset.

Reena asked the man and his wife what they thought of the movie, and they both said it illuminated the horrors of war, but it seemed the lesson was one we had yet to learn.

"It wasn't believable, though, was it? I mean a horse going through all that, everyone getting shot up around it, and then surviving?"

Reena had prepared to do battle with Mr. Furman and his overly-made-up, doting wife and she was not about to let that energy dissipate. She wanted more than a passing quip.

"I liked the super-realism in some of the shots," the woman said, "but, you know, the message is still the same even if it was Steven Spielberg's glossy version."

In her head Reena mocked the woman by repeating the words "super-realism" and "glossy version" and then speaking to her husband.

"As a man, what did you think of the horse…"

"… Joey, I believe his name was," the man said.

"All right then, Joey the horse. What did you think of that scene in the battlefield when it got all tangled up in barbed wire?"

"It was touching to see him struggling for his very survival and the horse's plaintive nickering brought tears to my eyes. I thought the animal was a metaphor for the world and the weary bondage of aggression."

"That horse would have been killed. They'd have just shot its legs out from under it. Used it for target practice. And when they finally got old Joey back home, he wouldn't have been worth a damn on the farm."

The couple told Reena good night, it was nice talking to her, and they proceeded out of the theater, arm in arm, without looking back.

"What about horse PTSD?" Reena said to no one in particular. "Nobody ever talks about that. Somebody should do a study on that issue."

BALANCE: $76

Saturday morning, before going for coffee, Reena searched on Craigslist for garage sales and jobs. The sales nearby listed things like mechanic's tools and freezers, baby clothes and used sofas, books and *National Geographics*, nothing she needed or wanted. For jobs it seemed like everything was either telemarketing, free internships, or sign spinning.

When she attempted to use the ATM, the machine showed she had multiple overdrafts and it kept her card. At coffee she tried to read the newspaper but had a hard time focusing, and her hands were shaking slightly. Reena was sitting at a table and two Filipino men asked if she would mind sharing because all the rest were full. She thought about it and said okay, as long as they didn't speak whatever language they spoke in the Philippines the whole time. The men found someplace else to sit.

Reena walked to Cherry Creek when she was finished and followed a path next to the water. It was a tranquil scene and she tried to get a glimpse of herself in the cloudy stream and nearly fell in. A homeless couple was just waking when she passed them and they asked if she had a cigarette and a dollar they could borrow. Don't have either, she told them, and pointed as though to begin a lecture, but waved them off.

Outside her condominium complex, on the street next to the sidewalk, she found an envelope with "Jerry M." written on the face and inside were two tickets. They were to the symphony that night and they were worth $38 apiece.

Reena thought for a moment about what decision to make. She could go to the symphony and enjoy herself, be with people who weren't worried about having been fired from an engineering company, or she could take the tickets back to the box office to try and get the money. She also considered standing outside before the performance and trying to sell just one of the tickets, keeping the other for herself. If nothing else, she could simply turn them in. It seemed serendipitous and like something positive was meant to happen.

That good news was overshadowed by the foreclosure notice taped to the door when she got back to the condo. It said she had 48 hours to pay the remaining HOA fees, or she would have to vacate the premises.

Reena thought she would get on the bus and go for a ride, try and figure out what to do, then probably redeem the tickets for cash. While she stood waiting at the stop, she watched the Indian couple across the street cleaning the rooms of their motel. When the woman thought no one was watching, she began dancing. Just before the bus came, she saw Reena and waved, and Reena waved back.

At the box office, Reena read the program notes that said the symphony that evening would feature an organ concerto by a French composer. She thought it sounded good, though she didn't know much about classical music. There was a short line and as she looked at people, successful and handsome, she wished she could attend the performance. Maybe something worthwhile would have come of it; she was sure something good would have come of it, but she definitely needed the money.

At the box office, before she showed her tickets, she asked the seller if it was possible to get a refund due to extenuating circumstances.

"Yes," the seller said, "what are the circumstances?"

"Illness," Reena said without hesitation.

"Oh," he said, "illness."

Reena thought she detected a measure of rudeness and after their transaction she would insist on speaking to the supervisor.

The seller asked to see the tickets and Reena was hesitant to give them up. She wanted to go to the symphony that night. Reluctantly she gave them to him and waited impatiently for the money. The seller scanned the tickets and looked for the results to appear on his screen.

"Illness," the seller said as a statement not a question.

"Yes," Reena said, "illness."

The seller stared at her and waited for her to say something more.

"These tickets belong to someone else, dear. They misplaced them and called us to reissue their tickets. Sorry. No illness, no tickets, no refund."

The seller made it a point to tear the tickets up in front of her and throw them away.

$117

Reena began the arduous walk home from downtown, maybe five miles, and she realized she hadn't worn her comfortable shoes. As she moved from block to block, she wondered if she should enroll in one of the programs that trained people for new jobs—she'd seen the billboards, or maybe go back to community college and learn a vocational skill, like pet grooming, small-engine repair, or esthetician.

When she was just halfway, she got blisters on the toes and heels of both feet, and they began to bleed. She took her shoes off and sat on a retaining wall. *To anyone driving by*, she thought, *I must be a sad sight.*

Reena didn't have the money to pay the HOA, and she wasn't going to get it any time soon, so she wasn't sure what to do next. She was going to have to take in boarders (but she didn't like them being in her condo), move into someone else's house (but what if she didn't like the smell of what they were cooking), or pack up a few changes of clothes, throw her valuables and toiletries in a case, scrounge up enough money for gas, put the cat in its carrying case, and go someplace. She didn't have any idea where. But someplace.

I'm underwater, she thought as she walked. *The place isn't that nice anyway; it isn't even worth what I paid for it; it's in the damn basement, and now they want to take it back. Hey, take it back, I can go and rent the same place around the corner for half the price, with a free introductory month.*

As she neared her building, Reena inquired at the places that had previously advertised $99 move-in rates or no deposit. The market has changed, she was told. The people who got dumped from their houses were all looking for apartments. Sorry, no more deals, and we're full anyway.

There were parking places in the open space that adjoined the creek that she could use short-term, just until she figured things out. She would lock the car doors at night and make a bed in the back seat, put most of her bags in the trunk.

That night she put some of her belongings in the car to try out camping. She found a spot out of the way and adjusted things here and there to make herself comfortable. Bowtie meowed throughout the night in her case, and Reena was hesitant to take her outside to go to the bathroom because she might run away.

About the time she began to drift off and hear her older brother from Indianapolis talking, someone banged on the window. She wished she had a German shepherd instead of a cat, and when she settled her nerves she got out and walked around the car. She clipped Bowtie's leash on her and the cat was wary of the new surroundings.

Just before dawn she turned on the radio, but was afraid she might run the battery down or run it out of the two dollars in gas she'd put in the tank. She listened to reggae for a time, music she hated, and then an interview with Bob Dylan as the sun came up. The best part of it, she thought, was hearing Joan Baez talking and singing, not Bob Dylan, and she had some suggestions for him about enunciation. Reena had always loved Joan Baez. The two singers sang a duet of "Blowing in the Wind," and Reena tried to remember the words and keep up.

At her condo, Reena walked slowly through the rooms. She was having a hard time seeing herself as the person who had been living there. A part of her was peeling away, she could feel it, not like her mental health, but like a layer of skin coming loose.

She tried to find enough money for coffee, including going through the ashtray in the car and shaking out the White House toy bank, but there was not enough, not even for half a cup at 7-Eleven. Reena drove to the engineering company and parked in the lot. She saw Mr. Furman's face on the building and got out and picked up a rock. She laughed at herself and stood there for a moment, then tossed the stone into the bushes.

A block away from her complex, the car ran out of gas and she managed to get it pulled over to the curb with only a little of it sticking out into the street. Anything she really needed she was going to get out of the condominium, store it in the car, and then that would be that. She would let the association have it, and they could deal with everything that was left behind.

Reena made sure she retrieved the right shoes this time, because she was positive she was going to have to do some walking. As she closed the door to her apartment, she wondered where she would stay the night and what she would do for food. She began walking in the neighborhoods nearby and occasionally stopped to look at the bigger houses. She liked to look at doors especially, well-designed doors, glass-paneled doors, rich-looking wood doors, and she walked up to some to touch them, rub them with her hands.

A woman came out while she was rubbing her hand on the face of an ornate oak door and asked what the hell she thought she was doing.

"I like doors," Reena said.

"Ah, that clears everything up. I had an expensive road bike that someone liked on the back porch. The police are on their way right now."

Reena started to say no, I mean, I really like doors and yours is nice but not so nice that you have to get worked up about it. Instead, she turned and hurried down the walk and out into the street. She began to run when the woman shouted that she was watching her, she was watching where she was going.

When she got to Colorado Boulevard she was out of breath. She could see the police car turning three blocks away and could imagine the woman pointing in the direction she thought Reena had gone.

The neon lights of the Bel-Care Motel were illuminated, and Reena walked through the parking lot to the office. She wanted to be inside somewhere quickly.

"Yes, may I help you?" the woman behind the counter said in lilting English. It was the same woman who had been dancing and waved to her. An Indian movie was playing on TV and

Reena was fascinated by it. The police cruiser pulled through the motel parking lot and stopped at the office. The Indian woman waved and the car continued on.

"This is a very famous star," the woman said about the TV. "Madhuri Dixit. And she lives here in Denver."

"A famous Indian movie star lives here?"

"Yes, the most famous, and her husband is a surgeon. She is from Mumbai, the same as me."

"What is the name of this movie?"

"*Aaja Nachle,* and it is my most favorite. Would you like to watch? She is great actress and also greatest dancer."

Reena sat in an upholstered chair next to the Indian woman who hummed along and held her arms up at the big dance numbers. Despite all the music, she had a hard time keeping her mind from wandering. They watched the movie in the small lobby and no customers came or went.

"Oh, I am so sorry," the woman said suddenly standing. "You are looking for room and I am forcing you to watch this Bollywood."

"That's all right," Reena said. "I'm in no hurry today."

"I have seen you before, yes? You are living nearby and maybe the pipes have broken in your apartment? Someone else is here today with same problem."

"There is a problem with my condo today, yes, that's right," Reena said, and she was trying to decide whether to tell the Indian woman about being evicted because of her HOA dues.

"I am giving you special price tonight. Three nights for $39 each. They will be finished by Monday, yes? And when you are not so tired, we will watch more movies."

Reena fished through her wallet to find her credit card. She was sure when the woman ran it, the company would reject it and she'd have to find shelter elsewhere. She laid the card on the counter.

"You are Reena?" the woman asked, reading her name. Reena nodded.

"I am Nisha," and she held out her hand and they shook.

"About the credit card," Nisha said, "it is acceptable for you to pay after two days or three. And if they are having the apartment fixed tomorrow, still special price."

The room was on the second floor, 201, which was also the date of her birthday in February. Reena thought it was lucky and considered it a good sign, though she had never been that much into signs and omens. She felt strange not having a suitcase or clothes to hang up, like an imposter and as if she were hiding out from the law. The room and the motel itself were in the one-star category, though everything worked and it was clean enough.

Reena stripped down to her underwear and left her clothes on the floor. She stood looking at herself, and in a chiding voice commented on her rippled knees. She crossed her arms over her breasts because she was getting cold and had a wave of prickled flesh. Then the shuddering came on and she couldn't control it. She pulled back the covers and wrapped her body tightly in the blanket and bedspread.

It's all right, Reena, she said, *it's all right.* And after a time, she fell asleep not knowing if things were truly going to be alright, or just alright for a few days. But she slipped off feeling like the Indian motel was the right place for her that night, and that seemed good enough.

Jana of Azerbaijan

The little girl's face looking out of the car window had unnerved Jana and she quickly stood to watch it pass. When she sat down she saw the face again and it triggered a memory of the times her family, she and her father and brothers, used to travel from Denver in their big sedan to Destin, on the Gulf. They would drive through the South to see her grandmother, her father's mother, every year for two weeks. Her own mother would stay home to "recuperate."

Jana had been sitting in the window of a coffee shop poking holes in a paper cup, thinking about her life, the recent past, but mostly how hard it had been over the last couple of years. She watched the sun move from left to right, across the window and the sidewalk. When a friend called and asked what she'd been doing with herself, she told her she'd been working on a memoir, and that was why she'd been spending time at this and other coffee shops. There were plenty of notes on the pages, ideas, even some kind of time frame for a memoir, but not much in the way of sentences or paragraphs yet.

One of the things Jana remembered so clearly from the trip was her father's hair, the smell of it, and that it was black and wavy. Standing behind him she would often stroke it, and he would murmur "that's my girl," or "you're the love."

She could see her brothers playing word games with billboards and highway signs and hear them squabbling while she knelt on the back seat and watched the road disappear behind them, her father driving, seemingly forever, and often late into the night. They mostly took the two-lanes and stayed at small, inexpensive motels, eating sandwiches in the car. The two boys slept together in one bed and she would sleep in the other with her father. To relax, he would read the newspaper at the table, and she would fall asleep to the soft sounds of drinking and pages turning. Sometimes she would wake during the night and find them intertwined.

That day, Jana put her hands around her coffee and tearfully whispered "Oh, Daddy" and then wrote down the names of her brothers, Karl and Dale, and underlined them.

Robert Jeppersen had visited that afternoon and they talked about what she was writing, any progress toward getting another job, the news from his office, and how the other Boys were doing. They never discussed his wife or children. He took her to dinner, at a salad buffet restaurant, and then they went back to the Bel-Care for the night. In the morning, when he left, he put a hundred dollars on the nightstand.

Jeppersen was one of three men who'd been attending to Jana since high school. The others were Harris Donaldson and Richard Levens. In high school she was a beautiful girl who had a way of shaking her hair out and allowing herself to be adored. They began the group when they were sophomores and she was a junior. Another boy, a fourth, Oster, moved away. It was Harris who started them off when he mentioned her vulnerability and her ankles and how perfect they both were. They would go on to discuss her fingers, lips, and breasts, and the unimaginable. The three followed Jana to college after they graduated and had been admirers and supporters through her marriages, jobs, disagreements with her son, and now, especially, because she had lost the house her mother gave her and had been staying at a motel.

The four had taken vacations to Vail and Cozumel and other places together, and the Boys all told their wives it was a special friendship from high school and college. They made it clear it was an arrangement they were going to keep, though. Sleeping with Jana, surprisingly, was not something the three pursued early on. In fact, they would've preferred the relationship as it was, worshipful, but once, when she was between her first and second husband and the quartet was in Santa Fe, they had to draw straws and Levens ended up sharing a room and then a bed with her. Donaldson and Jeppersen, to keep it in balance, started a few months later.

Regarding her house, Jana had been given a reprieve—she hadn't been making the refi payments—for a short period because there was confusion and her bank couldn't find the new mortgage, but they said she'd have to move at some point, maybe even on short notice, and until then she could stay. That day eventually came.

The day after she and Jeppersen were together, Jana had lunch with girlfriends at an Indian restaurant, near the motel. She enjoyed herself enormously, but she was distracted, more so than usual. She was hoping one of the other women would pick up the check because, after paying the motel bill, she was almost completely broke. She would have to make up something about forgetting her wallet or her credit card and then there would be the awkward moments that followed.

The waiter had written out separate checks for everyone when they were done, and when he came to Jana, he told her a gentleman had covered it. She looked around the dining room and asked which one.

"Just now gone," the waiter said, wagging his head, and

then pointed at the big window next to the door. She hurried to see if the payer was still there. A car was pulling away with a man driving and Jana rushed out to see if it was him. He was directly in front of the restaurant and she waved him down.

"Did you pay for my lunch?" Jana asked through the passenger window.

"Excuse me?" the man answered, dipping his head toward her.

Jana could see he didn't have the vaguest idea what she was talking about.

"Never mind," she said, and met her friends as they were coming out.

They escorted her to her car and on the driver's side window there was a sticky note.

"Didn't know if you'd remember me. Give a call and we'll have dinner. Keith Ammonds."

Keith Ammonds, Keith Ammonds, she said to herself. *The only Keith I can think of is from high school and the neighborhood.*

When she got to the motel, she waited until that evening and then called the number.

When Keith answered she absolutely could not place the voice. She asked if this was the person who left the note on her car and who paid for her meal.

"It is," he said. "Are you having a hard time remembering me?"

Jana apologized and said that she was. The only Keith she could remember was from growing up and that person was fifteen or sixteen at the time. She didn't say this but the one she remembered had been a pest, had asked her out repeatedly, and was unattractive.

"Same kid," he said. He told her he'd been infatuated with her as a boy and she could see his picture on Facebook. He was nice-looking now, even handsome, dressed in a sport coat and ironed shirt. They agreed he would come by a few days later and they would go to a nice restaurant—catch up.

In the morning she called Levens and asked if he remembered Keith Ammonds.

"I think he became some kind of chemist," and then he asked if she was really going to go on a date with him, because, he said as though joking, he wasn't sure the Boys would approve. Levens called later, as did Donaldson and Jeppersen, but she let the calls go to voicemail.

Jana decided to dress up, get her hair done, and she stopped at the Saigon Beauty College on west Mississippi because she'd heard they had discounted cuts, and she'd retrieved just enough quarters from the jar to pay for it. She normally would have gone to the shop next to the motel, but it had recently closed.

"Man Hair Cut, Ladie Hair Cut, All $6," it said in the window.

When she wandered in, the manager at the front counter wanted to know if he could help her, and she asked how well the students were trained.

"Very train," the manager said. "Some already working before in Vietnam."

"Do you have anybody who could cut my hair for a special event?"

"Walter available today. Very experience."

Walter was in one of the back booths shampooing his own hair and the manager called to him in Vietnamese. He finished and hurried to the front to introduce himself. He was short, tiny in fact, but the towel on his head made him look much taller.

"You have such shiny hair," Walter said, showing Jana to a chair.

"I just need my bangs shortened and a little on the ends trimmed, Walter," Jana said before sitting down. "You think you can do that? I have a special date with someone."

Walter said he could and began by massaging Jana's neck

and shoulders, which she allowed but wasn't quite comfortable with. He told her he was from a village outside Saigon and that he'd come to the city to be trained in his aunt's shop before emigrating. He'd only been in America for three years. Jana saw the story as a ploy to raise his tip.

"You so pretty, such shiny skin; you marry?"

"Am I married?" Jana repeated. She wondered if he meant now or had she ever been married. "Not currently. But I've had three along the way."

Walter asked what their names were and Jana paused before telling him.

"Mr. Celebrity, who thought he was a big shot and wasn't; Mr. Contractor, who built houses but wouldn't take care of mine; and Mr. Realtor, the last one, who lost all his money with the crash and didn't have any left for us."

Walter said yes, yes, as he cut her hair and pretended to understand everything she said. In response he told her all about living in America and everybody being so busy. He said he'd been attending community college and she asked what for.

"Computer," he said.

"How can you study computers when your English is so bad?" Jana asked, and wondered what Walter's real name was.

"My English pretty good now. Not so good three year ago."

Jana looked at her hair in the mirror and thought it seemed asymmetrical. She put her hand up to touch the sides and the back and Walter grimaced and rolled his eyes.

When he resumed he took the long scissors and began trimming close to her head. Walter looked away when another customer came in and during that moment of distraction, he cut the top of one of her ears. She didn't see or feel the trickle of blood initially, but when she did she screamed and jumped out of the chair.

Everything suddenly stopped at the college and other students rushed to see what the problem was.

Walter took the towel off his own head and tried to wipe Jana's blood with it. He managed to smear some on her face and clothes. When she saw what had happened she slapped him and ran out. Students and their customers lined up at the windows and in the door. The manager ran after her in the parking lot in an attempt to collect the six dollars she owed.

In the car rearview, Jana saw that her ear was still bleeding and it continued until she was able to pinch it off. She daubed a wad of saliva on the side of her face and around the parts of her ear, to clean them up with a tissue. There was a crimson stain the size of a medallion on the shoulder of her blouse, but she left it alone because she knew she could probably scrub it out later. On the way home she had to stop once to deal with the bleeding and while she waited she could see Walter chattering away in Vietnamese, explaining to the manager and other students what had happened.

There was only one car in the motel lot when she arrived, and she parked next to it. In her hurry to get to her room, however, and because her nerves were still in shambles from the college, she clipped the tail end of the vehicle. It was a bigger car, a luxury SUV, and Jana rationalized that that was the reason she'd hit it. No one was around to witness the accident, including the Indian couple who owned the Bel-Care, and so she decided in the short term to do nothing.

When she got to her room, Jana fell on the bed in her clothes. Moments later, though, she lurched up to check her ear in the mirror when she thought it might be bleeding. It hadn't bled again, but she sponged it with a washcloth, then put make-up on it and the cut was almost invisible. She wanted to rage at Walter, slap him repeatedly and call him obscene names, but she was too busy thinking about Keith.

After her shower and before she dressed for her date, Jana brushed her dark brown hair and shook it out like she had in high school. She posed and swung her hair and hips seductively, feeling almost as good as when she was seventeen.

That night Keith arrived late and it was clear he'd been drinking. He asked about the motel and she explained how the bank had taken her house after missing a few payments and that she had just not had the energy to rent an apartment. The motel gave her a discount and they were nice to her, so she put the big things she wanted to keep in a neighbor's garage and moved in. There was a clothesline strung across the room, but Jana had taken all of her lingerie down and stuffed it in a drawer.

In Keith's new car they drove to an upscale Thai restaurant. Jana was not fond of this type of Asian food, and had it not been their first date, she would have requested a change.

Jana talked about her three husbands, one of whom Keith knew, the Jana Boys, all of whom Keith remembered, and her estranged son, who was now living in Emeryville with his unattractive girlfriend. When Keith attempted to explain what he did as a chemist and the difficult path to getting his doctorate, Jana listened for a few minutes and then changed the subject. She had a third glass of wine and asked rhetorically why she was unable to get a job at her level and why so many foreign people had such good jobs.

Because it was a beautiful evening, Keith drove them around the city with the windows down and stopped at Washington Park. Jana initially refused to get out of the car, but after some coaxing they wandered past the big playground and stood in the old boat house. There were many couples strolling, some walking their dogs.

Keith pointed out the lone pelican on the lake amidst the geese and egrets. He showed her the night herons on a sandbar, who stood poised to spear any little fish that happened by, and the ancient cormorants perched high in the trees with their wings draped. When he held her arm as they walked, she let him, but she didn't know what to make of the nature tour.

Jana could see Keith watching her whenever she spoke and it made her uncomfortable.

"Do you ever look back and think about the person you were and the person you've become?" Keith asked. "I mean, think about who we are now, how we've grown and changed, our paths."

Jana considered Keith's question and didn't know how to respond. She was never comfortable talking about her personal psychology, especially with people she didn't know that well. And she didn't want to talk about the rough period she was in, or she might start crying.

"What about you, Keith? You're working for a corporation as a chemist. You probably have a lot of responsibility."

But Keith ignored her question. "I mean, doesn't there come a time in a person's life when they just have to put the defenses down and say this is who I am, okay, a little rough around the edges, but this is me. Not that we can't continue to learn things, change, you know, get better, but…"

They were sitting on a park bench and Jana looked at Keith without responding.

"What are you thinking about, Jana?"

"Today I went for a haircut at the Saigon Beauty College. I like to help those people out whenever I can. I didn't think I was going to tell you this, but while I was there, the beautician—if that's what you call a man—the beautician, Walter, with a big towel on his head, cut my ear."

"The guy at the beauty college cut your ear? Bad or just a little?"

"I thought I'd have to have stitches," she said. "And it must have been near a vein because it bled, it really bled. I almost passed out driving."

Keith motioned for Jana to show him the cut and she obliged by lifting the hair away from her ear. The make-up covering the wound had rubbed off and he could see that the nick had already started to scab.

Softly Keith put his hand in her hair and smelled it. He looked as though he enjoyed Jana this way and kissed her on the temple. She shook her hair out, licked her lips, and closed her eyes. She could see this turned him on—no doubt reminding him of the way he used to feel in high school. They sat together for a time and when it began to get cool, Keith led Jana back to the car and opened the door for her.

When she got out of the car at the Bel-Care, Jana saw Nisha, the owner of the motel, and they waved at each other and paused as though they were about to speak. But when neither did, they nodded, smiled, and continued on their way.

At the motel, Jana invited Keith to come up and he followed her. There was a folded piece of paper taped to her door, and she had an idea what it was about. She looked around the parking lot and then went in.

In the room, Keith took his sport coat off and threw it on the bed. He flopped down on top of it and kicked off his shoes.

"I have a chance to go to Azerbaijan with my company," he announced. "Do consulting work in one of their refineries. Pay would be double and they'd cover all expenses. I'm thinking about going. Know where Azerbaijan is?"

Jana tried the name out in her mouth and when she couldn't think of where it was or one thing about it, she said, "No, no idea."

"The company will allow me to bring a spouse or significant

other. They tell me Baku is a beautiful old city, pretty nice. Ever think about going someplace like that?"

Jana had to stop for a moment and ask herself: *Is he asking me to go abroad with him or just speaking in general?*

"When is this? When are you going?"

"They want me to be there June 18. It's right on the Caspian Sea."

"Keith, are you asking if I want to go with you?"

"Jana, it could be an interesting change. Seems kind of sudden, I know, but it would give you a chance to get away from this motel for a few weeks. Give us a chance to get to know each other. And hey, could be a lot of fun too."

Jana lay down next to Keith and before long they were both asleep. But in the middle of the night he got up and took off his clothes. She let him take hers off and then they made love. He woke her at around five and they made love again. When she fell back asleep she wandered in another country, a sandy country with women wearing scarves.

When she woke for the final time, Keith was propped on an elbow looking at her.

"What happened, Jana?"

"What happened with what?"

"The Jana I knew in high school was different, full of life, curiosity, energy."

"People change, you know, things happen. I've had a bad year, and I don't need somebody reminding me of it."

Jana got up, went into the bathroom, and closed and locked the door. She turned on the shower but didn't climb in. She only wanted the white noise to cover the sound in her head. *Who is this Keith to say something like that to me? Oh, stop it, stop talking like that.* "He adores you, so why not go, Jana," she said out loud, but became irritated. "What do you have here? You're staying in a motel run by foreigners, with no Internet and no job, and your friends are immature men you've known since high school."

She wanted to look at herself and wiped the mirror over and over, but to no avail. Jana ran her fingers through her mangled hair and then gripped the sink.

"Keith," she said as she opened the door, "Keith." She was smiling but Keith was gone and the door to the room was open. There were two twenty-dollar bills tossed on the night-stand and when Jana saw them she began to sob.

"No," she said trembling, "no, no."

Jana lay down on the bed and fell back asleep. When she woke, around noon, she tried to call Keith. She tried several more times and only got his voicemail. Jana went online at the library and began searching for information on Azerbaijan. *I could go there,* she said to herself, swallowing hard, *I've never traveled, but I could visit there, especially after seeing pictures of the old capital. And Keith would love it if I went with him.*

By evening, when Keith hadn't called, she tried phoning each of the Boys—Robert Jepperson, Harris Donaldson, and Richard Levens, but none of them picked up. She wanted to tell them about Keith's offer and that she might be going to Azerbaijan.

Jana opened the note that had been taped to her door. It was the person downstairs whose car she'd bumped. He threatened that if she didn't contact him and give him her insurance company's name, he would call the police and report a hit-and-run.

But Jana was happy and nothing could dissuade her. She thought of Keith's Facebook picture and saw the two of them strolling together next to a seawall in a European city. She had spoken to the universe and the universe had answered.

In the morning she would begin sorting the things she would require for the trip. She knew to travel light because all the magazines said she could buy much of what she needed from outdoor markets and avoid the airline baggage charges.

Then she began thinking of things she could teach the people, whatever it was they called themselves, like English to the children. She would bring trinkets for babies and household items for the women. She would get books and surprise Keith by learning some of the language. And while he worked during the day, she would go off in the city or the countryside.

Karen of the EZ-Life

1.

Soto was somewhere else first and then moved the lounge here. King Soopers down the street, the beauty shop on one side, and the motel. I came over from the Kentucky Inn twenty-two years ago. He was there one day and said let's play some shuffleboard. I was kicking his little Mexican butt and he put his hand on my ass. I looked at him and said you ever touch me like that again and I'll break your fucking nose.

That turned out to be the largest joke. I went to work here and let him and most of south Denver put their hands on my skinny tush, inside and outside this place. I read these women's magazines in the grocery store and get the biggest bang. Ten tips to make him want you. How to take charge in the bedroom. Like I need one of those magazines to tell me it's okay to get laid? Every chance I get to jump men or boys I take it. No help needed.

I've been seeing Laughing Man for nearly two years, but that doesn't mean a whole hell of a lot. His real name is Burl, but I call him Laughing Man because everything I say he laughs at. He screws me and he's laughing. I tell him a joke and he can't stop laughing. Hear the one about the rat who goes into a bar and says if I show you a really good trick will you give me a free drink? I don't finish and Burl is howling up a storm.

First night together I learned that Laughing Man had a crooked dick. He slid that thing in me and it went around the corner and touched something. I heard Michael Jackson and Roy Orbison at the same time. I get to thinking about Burl's dick and next thing you know I'm in the ladies' restroom with my skirt up. The morning after the first time, Burl said don't tell anybody. He meant about his dick. That day I told everybody. He was here five minutes and Soto asked to see his dick. He looked at me and said damn you, Karen.

Burl goes out of town on business at least once a month. He's got the western territory for medical devices like colostomy bags, urinary leg bags, all kinds of incontinence products. He goes away, I find a fill in. Before Burl it was Teddy. Before Teddy it was Sanchez. Before Sanchez it was Terp. One of them's not busy, I call or say something if they're here.

I'm almost sixty now. A couple years I'll be getting Social Security. Hard to believe. When I got here I was thirty-seven. My tits weren't saggy and I didn't have lines in my face. Now my arm muscles droop and my waist is lumpy and headed for both coasts.

And this whole thing, the EZ-Life, definitely isn't what I had in mind when I started out. I got a degree in psych, which I learned is another way of saying I'd be doing call-center work or nights at an orphanage. First job I got I went to work with one of those loser corporations that was firing people out the back door and hiring them in the front.

That was also the first one to cut me loose. The very next week I went to work at a place that made me a special offer: more responsibility, less money. How could I pass that up? The world's largest producer of mozzarella. One of the bosses came around in the second week and asked me if I wouldn't mind dipping my tits in the cheese vat. No problem froggy, I told him, long as you jump in there holding your magic wanger.

Here's a question for Google: What's the deal with men and tits? Every woman knows that if you unbutton your blouse a couple buttons, and they're halfway nice, you can walk into NORAD without being asked a question. They're tits, I want to yell out. Tits. Fleshy fat things. Jesus fucking Christ, get over it.

I like men a lot, though, despite their faults and distractions. Always have. My father used to work for the power company as a line inspector and I'd ride around with him. We'd stop for sandwiches or cheeseburgers somewhere; he'd have a schooner and a shot, talk with his friends. I thought I was so big then and the men treated me special, like I was a grownup, and Grandpa gave me my own hardhat. He never had to say anything to me; I just knew when he didn't like something or he wanted me to get in the truck. And he would wink at me right in the middle of a conversation. I loved that.

Women, I hate to say this, are whiners for the most part, and they like to talk about hair and how pretty somebody's outfit is. Most of my women friends are these other gals like me, who work at bars during the day. They have old-timey names: Dot, Toots, Bootsie, Babs, bartender names. Smokers, with raspy voices.

But if you want to meet the model for a whiner, be here at five when Larry comes in. He's one man I have never fucked. And don't plan to. I said five but lately it's been five-thirty or quarter till. I don't have any reservation about getting on his case either.

"Did Soto send out a memo and I didn't get it, Larry?"

"What? What are you talking about, memo?"

"The one that says come in any fucking time you want. The one that says you don't have to clean the fucking grill after your shift. The one that says if you run out of beer in one of the taps, you don't have to pull another keg out of the cooler. That memo." Larry Conover is his name, but the regulars call him Larry Combover.

Part of my job is to order up any supplies we need, all the alcohol, kegs, meat, make the chili, and fix whatever Larry fucks up. Plus now Soto has started serving dogs steamed in beer. I don't know if I can handle it. Next thing people will be coming in here in coats and ties.

And that brings up another issue: Soto doesn't hardly come in anymore. He's off driving around the country in his little pickup. He'll call me from Elko or North Platte or Cape Girardeau. Called me last night from Vermillion, wanted to know how it was going, what the deposit was, if I'd been ripping him off. He laughs after he says it. I tell him you're not making enough here to steal. Just kidding, just kidding, he says, I know you're not the kind of person who'd dip into the till.

Which isn't true anymore. I wasn't ever into that until he asked me one too many times. When I count both drawers out and make the deposit, I take fifty bucks now no matter what, right off the top. And Larry, that smart son-of-a-bitch, he thinks he's getting away with something. Every day when I count him out, he's always over. He thinks because he's twenty or twenty-five over, no problem, better to be over than under. Of course what that means is he's shorting somebody at the bar or he's losing track of what he's stealing or he's giving his buddies free drinks and throwing some of the tip money in there because he feels guilty.

Soto dresses and looks like Buffalo Bill Cody. Mustache and chin beard, leathers with fringe, a big flat-brimmed cowboy hat. He goes into bars in these towns and tells stories about how Buffalo Bill was a scout and buffalo hunter, how he was a stagecoach driver and worked for Pony Express. He's done it in here pretty often and you can tell when he's bullshitting, just making stuff up about old Bill.

One of these guys told me not long ago that I moved around behind the bar like I was a boat on the ocean, and I thought at first he meant it like I glided along, that I was smooth, and that it was a compliment. I said, well, thank you honey. But I got to thinking about it and realized maybe he saw me more like a ship of bones, like one of those tall-masted ones, and that my skin looked like the billowy sails. I haven't been eating that much lately. Just not hungry. And not ever salads.

Once in a while, Nisha, the Indian woman from the motel, will come and get change when she runs out. Almost nobody pays for a motel these days with cash, though, or if they do you know what they're up to. She sometimes brings me things to eat, like lentils or cauliflower or spinach or their special kind of chicken. I can't put anything in my stomach until after I've had a few drinks. I've tried to get her to taste our chili, but she's vegetarian. Rajiv isn't but she is.

Think about coming all the way from there, she was raised in one of the big cities I can't remember the name of, and landing here in Denver, on Colorado Boulevard, and owning a motel. At least they can speak the language. It was her husband's idea. He borrowed the money from his family and bought it sight unseen. And I have to tell you this: the people who had it before, the Lewistons, they didn't take care of it. Deferred all the maintenance while they watched TV and ate Doritos. But Nisha's different; she's always working on something.

Their families introduced them when they were twelve or a young age like that, imagine. Nisha and Rajiv, and when she dresses up she's a doll, a regular princess. She wears one of those things on her forehead all the time, a bingee or bungee, as a decoration and to show she's a married woman.

She told me once when we were talking, in America mattresses and bras always on sale, and she moved her head in this really cute way. Sometimes when I've had too much, or I find a boyfriend I don't want to take to my house or go to his, I stay with Nisha. She never asks any questions when I call over, just hands me the key. And she has never had a drink in her life and only been with one man. I told her, I'm covering for you on both counts, Nisha, don't worry about it.

Sometimes when I wake up in the early morning and I'm there, it takes me a minute to remember where I am and who it is that's next to me. Half the time it's nobody and then I start to worry, and I think was there somebody here and they left?

A guy came in one day; I like to call him My Angry Young Man. Still comes around occasionally. He was very handsome, in that rugged kind of way. I thought he was going to rob the place. Maybe he was at first and then decided not to. We got to talking and I fixed him something to eat, a nice burger and a bowl of chili. He told me he'd been in prison and couldn't find work. I asked him what he was good at and he said cars. Seems like there's a need for that, I said. But he said something about people being able to tell he'd been in the joint, almost from a distance.

We talked even after Larry got here and then went back to his place. I could tell he was into something. Inside his house he had all kinds of random shit stacked up, and he had cars parked up on the lawn with the driver's side window broken out.

We went on like that for a while, his house, my house, six weeks. I was starting to get attached. One night we got wasted and decided to spend the night at the motel. I woke up at around three or four with him looking at me, and he had all of his clothes on.

"What's going on, Tony?" That was his name, and he was upset. My girlfriends had already told me to watch out, be careful, especially after I told them about the cars in the yard.

"You're starting to shrivel up," he said. "Everywhere, all over, even down there."

"I'm fifty-nine, Tony, what'd you expect?"

"I can't believe I've spent this much goddamn time with you."

I started to cry, I don't know why. I should have just told him to fuck himself and get out, like I do everybody else. But I couldn't.

I asked him to sit on the bed for a minute, talk with me. But he stood up and paced back and forth.

"Come on, Tony," I said, "come back to bed. It'll be alright."

He picked up one of the chairs and smashed it against the wall. If I'd done or said anything I thought there might have been violence, that he'd beat me up.

"You got any motherfucking money?" he yelled.

"Sure, a few bucks. Bring me my purse."

But he grabbed it and went through it, throwing everything out. I had about fifty dollars that I'd kept from the drawer.

"I'm afraid if I spend any more time with you I'll catch it; I'll start to look like you."

He stuffed the money in his pants and turned to open the door. Then he walked back and kicked the bedpost. He wanted to rage at me but didn't know what to say. His face and eyes were swollen. His nose was running and he'd started to cry.

He slammed the door behind him and immediately came back in.

"Karen," he said with his teeth clenched; he was shaking. He held up his fists before suddenly dropping them. Then he went out and slammed the door for the final time.

2.

Soto had been off on one of his trips. He sleeps in the back of the truck, in the camper. He'd gotten up to Montana and had made day excursions over into Canada. He said on the phone that the border patrol on their side messed with him, made him put his outfit on and do his spiel, then went through the vehicle. And he told me he was bringing somebody back with him.

First thing I thought was he'd picked up a hitchhiker, a guy who had a thousand road stories. Maybe a crusty old fellow with a beard and slits for eyes.

He got off the interstate and came right here. As if to show us the catch he had in his creel. Soto had his nose wide open, that was for sure, I could see it right away.

"Everybody," he said, "everybody. I'd like you to meet Connie Clendenny. She's a Montana girl looking to make a new start here. She'll be staying with me for a brief time until she can establish herself."

Soto went from table to table and up to the bar introducing her to people; Mercer, this is Connie; Elfland, this is Connie; Turner, this is Connie. I assumed she must've had royal blood the way he was escorting her around the room.

And when he finally got to me he had a smile so wide I should've known something was up. "Connie," he said, holding her elbow, "this is Karen, our number one bartender and all-around person."

"Oh, Karen," she cooed, "Soto talked practically the whole way here about you and how important you are to the EZ-Life Lounge."

"That Soto," I said, "I'm sure you meant when he wasn't talking about himself he was talking about me."

Connie was like Burl; she laughed at everything. More like a kind of tittering, though, with her hand pinching her bottom lip. But Soto didn't think what I said was that funny.

"Connie's going to start helping out a little from time to time, spell you guys, work the grill when you get busy."

She was definitely cute enough and a few of the soldiers in the barracks would have liked to have jumped her after Soto was done with her.

"Ever work in a fast-paced, up scale place like this, Connie?" I said.

"Well, not exactly. But I've been waiting tables at the Big Sky for a few years and that's where Soto met me."

I started off helping her find her way around. She'd never poured a glass of beer, so I showed her. Didn't know the basic drinks, like Manhattan or vodka martini. Had to show her how to make our top-notch chili and how to give the grill a quick cleaning. She wasn't a real-fast learner, but she was okay.

For a while there, after Tony left, I fucked everybody. Everybody except Burl. And Soto. And Larry, of course. He hurt my feelings, My Angry Young Man. I have to say it. I tried to blow it off, that little prick, but it didn't go away so easily.

I'd like to be able to travel like Soto. More than just next door to the motel. And not in a pickup with a camper shell. A nice big car, not the beater I have. Stay in hotels with a good boyfriend. Eat something besides burgers and chili.

Mondays we should probably close anyway. If we make three-hundred dollars, it's a good day. So when Soto asked if I wanted to take a break, get a little relief, let her sit in on Monday, I said sure, why not. This was a month after Connie started work. Think she's ready? he asked. Ready as she'll ever be, I told him.

I didn't come near the place that day; didn't call either.

Next day she told me she made a hundred in tips. And from then on she started wearing blouses so low you could read the washing instructions on her bra. Soto wondered if we should start opening on Sundays for the games; we'd normally only been open Monday through Saturday.

Who's going to work it? I asked him. Connie, she wants to do it, he said.

"And we could make Mondays a regular deal," he added.

"No problem," I said, "long as you put me on salary same as six days." I'd been working six days a week, Monday through Saturday.

"Oh, I don't know, Karen. We got all this new overhead, expenses, and I'm thinking about making some other changes, bigger menu."

That was about the same time Soto asked me why a woman my age wore tights to work every day.

"Jeans, why not jeans?" he said. "They would be all right with a nice shirt."

Fucking Soto. Not exactly a closet diplomat.

One of the guys told me Connie had a kid back home that she sent money to. I asked her and she showed me pictures. Cute boy, stays with her parents. I asked if she'd been to school, if she had any college, and she said she was trying to finish her G.E.D. online.

"Sometimes it feels like I have to scratch and claw for everything," she said. "You know how it is, don't you, Karen?"

She liked to say my name whenever we talked. Karen this and Karen that. Maybe that's the way they talk in Montana.

Not too long ago Soto and I had a few minutes when no one was here. He asked if I had any money put away, if I had any retirement.

"Shit," I said, "I don't even own my own house. And the little I'm going to get from SS, I'm going to have to keep working here till you scoop me up and put me in the Dumpster."

Soto shook his head.

"How about you take a week at Glenwood, on me. Wouldn't hurt you to take a good break. And you used to like the hot springs up there. Remember that?"

"I'd love to take a break, Soto," I said, looking straight at him. "But I'm afraid when I got back somebody else would be here in my place."

This was about the same time Tony started coming around again. I didn't even want to talk to him because I knew what would happen. And then I figured out what to do.

"Connie," I said one day when they both were there. "Have you had a chance to meet Tony?"

Right away they started up. I could see the sparks. And she moved out of Soto's palace and into Tony's used car lot over night. You'd think Soto would've made a fuss, fired her, and I think he thought about it, but a couple days later he had another one in the bar that he was kissing and loving on.

I asked Soto if his offer was still good, Glenwood Springs.

"Yeah, I guess so," he said. "Sure, why not."

I spent the whole week walking the town, swimming in the hot pool, and didn't drink a drop of alcohol. They have an old Penney's store there and I bought a new pair of jeans one day and came back and bought another one the next.

I felt pretty good when I got home.

Only thing, Connie was working all my shifts, and Soto had given me hers.

"Problem?" Soto said.

"No problem," I said. "Sunday and Monday are perfectly fine by me." I wanted to say, perfectly fucking fine, asshole, even a dipshit knew that was going to happen, but I held back. And between the new jeans and a decent-looking top, with a few giveaways on my part, I made about half as much as I'd been making, but in just two days. Plus I didn't have to cook any chili or clean up after Larry.

Tony started showing up on Sunday, talking to me about his life and about Connie. He was working at a yard dismantling cars way south. Sounded like a chop shop to me, which I asked him, but it was working outside doing something he knew how to do, so what can you say.

I didn't want to talk to him about Connie because a part of me was still in love with that beautiful convict, but I had an idea something was going to happen.

Connie had already started covering up the bruises and handprints, and she would say things to me in passing like whew, that Tony has a temper, doesn't he.

"A big load," I said to him one day.

"What's a big load?"

"I'm proud of you, Tony."

"Fuck yourself, Karen. What the hell are you talking about?"

Tony had gotten another tattoo on his neck.

"All that responsibility you're taking on. It's a lot."

"She's just staying at my house till she gets her own place."

"Seems like she's got a different idea. Like she's getting starry-eyed."

"I know why you're doing this, Karen. You're still upset I walked out. Tell the fucking truth."

"Connie ever tell you about sending money back to Montana?"

"She's helping her parents out. They have medical problems. One of these days we're going to drive up there."

"Maybe you can bring the boy back with you."

"What boy? She have a younger brother she's responsible for?"

"Cute kid. Ask her to see the pictures. It's her son, Tony. She's got a kid up there."

Tony turned on the bar stool as though he were going to run out the door. He chugged the tumbler of beer in his hand, then stood up and smashed the glass on the floor.

"She never said nothing about no kid in Montana, just mom and dad. And we ain't bringing nobody back with us, that's for damn sure."

"I never should have said anything, Tony. Sorry, I thought you knew."

Tony stormed out the door cursing Connie and me and everyone who was there staring at him.

"What did you say to him?" Soto asked me on the phone.

It was Monday morning and I was at the bar. I knew he was talking about Tony.

"What did I say to who?"

"He beat her up. She's in the hospital. Something you said to Tony got him pretty pissed off."

"I told him I was still in love with him. Do you think that's what did it?"

"Goddamnit Karen. Now who's going to work Tuesday through Saturday?"

"I've really begun to enjoy Sunday and Monday, Soto. All those years I didn't realize what I was missing during the rest of the week. I'd forgotten what the sun looked like."

I knew what he was going to say and sure enough he did— Tuesday about ten.

"Karen, look, Connie's still in the hospital and I don't have anybody to take her place."

"No kidding, Soto. That sounds serious. Connie's still in the hospital? Where will she stay when she gets out?"

"Probably with me. Goddamn Tony. They're looking for him. You never should have said whatever you said to him, Karen."

"Geez, I'm not sure, Soto. I got things scheduled. I'd have to call my friends and cancel lunch. They'd be upset."

"Christ almighty, Karen. Can't you help me out today? After all, you're partly to blame."

"Oh, I don't know, Soto. Partly to blame, huh? You didn't forget how to mix drinks and pour beer, did you?"

Soto left messages throughout the day, but I ignored them. He offered me my old shift back, with an increase in salary. Then called saying he'd fired me completely. Then called and apologized, pleaded with me. Then called to tell me I shouldn't have done that to Connie.

I'll think about it overnight, Soto, possibly.

I made another reservation for Glenwood Springs, three days. Not sure what I'll do all that time. Go to a movie. Maybe hike, read. I haven't done either of those two things since college. I could see myself living in the mountains, having big dogs, sitting around campfires.

Definitely not with Burl, though.

Who knows? Maybe I'll try to scare up Tony, take him on a long drive.

Might even find a new boy, one along the way.

Or go on the damn trip by myself, call Soto from different towns.

Hard to say.

Sippy
and the Appropriations

We were renting from Engle when we got started. Both of us out of work, just roommates. One day Engle walked away from his big house, told us to send our part of the rent to Albuquerque. And we said yeah, for sure, you bet, Engle, take care. He was five minutes gone and we said like hell.

We didn't have it to send anyway.

I'm jumping ahead a little, but when you're famous or you're a criminal, I learned, the one thing you've got a lot of is time in between gigs. Putt-putt golf, shopping in the middle of the day, working out occasionally, store openings, checking the Internet, naps. I became gluten-free and learned I had an allergy to chickpeas. That's what the woman at the vitamin store said.

Chickpeas?

Something told me Ralston was knocking these branch places over, but he never said anything, and he hadn't gotten caught. We'd started midnight strolling by then—his room, my room. Which was a switch for me—men. I'd only had girlfriends for a while.

He had a couple close calls he said later, but they missed him both times. He'd been going off in the afternoon once every couple months and coming back with money. But I knew he wasn't doing day labor. And I think maybe Engle helped him sometimes.

I had a little saved back from the corporation but was running out. Ralston, however, was always broke, especially in between his visits.

He was the one that got me started. After I'd been going on my own I thought if the cops ever grabbed me I'd say I was under his spell. He made me, officer. Forced me at gunpoint. And then I just kept on, your honor, because I was too afraid to stop. If they bought that, I had some ground at Yucca Flat I needed to cut loose for cheap.

Ralston. One day he said help me out, Sippy. How about you let me take your car? I knew better than to loan Ralston my car. I wondered why he had his all locked up in the garage and what he was up to. But I got the idea then, too. Take my car where? I said. He was doing these little credit unions that were tucked away. They'd seen his car and there was even a story in the paper: The alleged getaway vehicle was a green Subaru station wagon. Ralston's. He'd parked in the neighborhood.

"What we gonna do, Ral?" I said to him.

"You know what I'm getting ready to do, Sippy."

"What's your chances of getting us caught?"

"Not high," he said. A Bible college savings and loan in a shopette out in Lakewood. I drove but was nervous as hell. He walks in and comes back out with thirty-five hundred seventy-three dollars. They were counting on the Lord protecting them and Ralston was counting on them counting on that too. I stepped on it and touched a two-hour parking pole with the bumper. He told me *slow, slow, Sippy. Ain't nobody comin' after us.*

And when we got back he was happy as all get out—joking around, steak on the grill, and a big bag of credit union money on the table. Then he opened it. Christian folks but they weren't totally stupid. He pulled out the first bundle of bills and then that damn dye went everywhere, especially on his face when he looked down in it. He used bleach and that goopy stuff mechanics use on their hands. There was still some on his cheek and by his eye and he told people it was a birthmark when they asked.

That money wasn't any good, by the way. Nobody takes red money and the Federal Reserve will reject it.

"Let's fly out to San Francisco," he said one day. "If we like it we'll move out there."

"Yeah, sure," I said, "why not." I was thinking when we got back I'd dump him because I was getting tired of looking at his red face and he'd been teasing me a lot about my caboose, as he called it, which I didn't like. And I was thinking about the ladies again.

The mortgage company had been around looking at Engle's house to repo it.

"What'll we use for money?" I said. We had a garage sale and sold off all Engle's stuff—his furniture, lawn mower, appliances—everything but the microwave. We had enough for the plane tickets, but not any to spend on food or a motel.

"No problem," Ralston said. "I got a place I'm going to visit."

In the morning he goes off to get coffee while the airport van is coming. Plenty of time, plenty of time. The van gets there, we wait and wait. I tried his cell three, four times. You know what happened, right? Ran out of lives while he was off getting coffee and making a stop.

But here's the thing: I learned something from Ralston the day we were at the Christian S&L. Aside from the excitement. Places like credit unions, even though they're not banks, as soon as you get one, they're on alert. They talk to each other. This last one before the trip they were looking for him. They knew his car. They got wise.

And I was hooked.

*

Walgreens. That's where I started. And I'm normally one of their best customers. I even buy groceries there sometimes when it's late. The one by the house, the people are the nicest. So I just went to the other one down the street. No, that's okay if the package is open, we'll take it back. Did you notice that vitamin C's on sale two for one? Oh, I think that's a lovely shade of lipstick on you.

My number one rule: Only visit places you know. Except if it's right by your house like Walgreens. You'd think I'd say only go with the places you don't like, where they tried to rip you off or the hostess was rude to you. No. You're a lot less nervous and you've got a clear mind. The thing of it is, you just have to make sure you dress right. And you're not going to get a big pile of cash like you would from a bank or savings and loan.

I start with what I call my foundation. And it all comes from Goodwill. A nice wig first. Not blond. I try to look as much like a Mennonite as I can. Plain, plain. A blouse that doesn't show much neck or boob and isn't too frilly. A skirt that's a dark gray or navy. Sensible shoes.

When they ask the witnesses later, I want them to be confused by my plainness. I want them to not be able to remember what I looked like. And unattractive glasses, which I get at Goodwill too.

There was a story in the paper a month ago after I'd been in Taco John's. One of the employees said I was tall and attractively dressed; the other thought I was short and looked kind of dumpy. She used the word dumpy in the article. But that's what I'm talking about.

And here's the greatest thing: Sometimes I ditch my stuff and come right back. While the cops are still there. What happened? I ask. They tell me about the woman who just robbed the place. No kidding, I say. A woman robbed this place? What did she look like? About half the time they can't remember or they get it so wrong.

Before I get into the next step and what I do to get ready, I want to mention the college student who reported I'd gotten twenty-five hundred dollars. This was at the salad place on Colorado Boulevard. I figured out he gave me fifteen-hundred and kept part of it. I went back when he was on duty and no one was around. Twenty-five hundred, hunh? He knew it was me. I must have miscounted, I said. You better get out of here, he said. I'll call the cops. I got on the cell and told him I was going to report a robbery. The one where he stole a thousand dollars. Okay, okay, he said. What do you want? Nothing, I said, but I might need dinner one of these days.

Second thing I do is my walk-around. At the other Walgreens, not the one by the house, I've looked around that place from the alley out to the street, the parking lot, and the quickest way to get the hell away from there when it's over. Sometimes I walk. Other times I've got the car around the side and facing the right direction, tape distorting the numbers on the license plates. Once I got on the bus, rode it two stops, and got off. And if there are any surprises, which there have been a few, I want to have some idea about that too and what I'll do.

Here's an example: There was a time at Sears, I came out the door after I'd made a withdrawal and the police were parked outside with their guns drawn. Shit, I said, shit. Get the hell out of the way lady, they yelled, get down. There was a guy who'd tried to rob the First Colorado Bank next door and ran into Sears. He was hiding inside. By the time they got into the store he was long gone out the back. He made it easy for me. When they couldn't find him the employees told them they'd just been robbed. The cops were all confused. They thought the escapee had robbed the store. No, no, they said, a tall lady who was kind of plain looking, she robbed us and went out when you were coming in. I could've been in the next state by then.

Anyway, the point is: look the place over real good.

Three. If you can do it, go inside about the time you were thinking of committing your felony. Do they keep all the cash in the drawer, or is some down below? Aside from two o'clock in the morning, when is the best time? Here's a good approach I use. Buy something cheap and hand them a hundred-dollar bill. You'll see if their money is down below or the manager has to be called to bring it from the back. We don't have change for a hundred, the clerk told me the other day. Oh, well, I'll just have to put everything back then. I had bar soap, lotion, deodorant, pads, and he knew if I didn't put it back he'd have to. He pulled the cash box out from down below and broke my hundred. Then I asked for the rest of the money that was in there.

I've started thinking of the robberies as "appropriations." I'd like to say I'm only doing it because of the one-percenters, but that's B.S. I'm doing it because I don't have a job and I'm not going to get one. I'm 46. How did I even get here and not have steady employment or a house or kids and a husband, or a long-term girlfriend? Hard to say, and I'd rather not talk about it.

It's scary for a woman not to be someplace secure. More than for a man. What's my fallback position? I realized that's why women kiss up so much. They're afraid and it's better to be in a lousy situation than be out on the street when you could've kissed up a little and stayed.

I had a friend once, Froda. She worked at one of the big banks whose name starts with Wells. Just a teller, but she could count money. Fast. And she spoke Spanish. The branch manager asked her to lunch. Then another time. He probably had a thing for thick ankles, because Froda had thick ankles. He let her know as a college grad she could move up the ladder if she had dinner with him. And of course he was married. Three weeks after she got the promotion they sent her home. She was in international wire transfers and they moved all that somewhere else, the Philippines.

Ralston left me something else too, a gift. Part of the franchise. Told me he never once had to take it out. I guess they just took his word for it. It's what he carried in the small of his back at the top of his pants. A girly Bersa. Fits right in my bag. When we were going to San Francisco, Ralston left it at home. I'd never carried a gun, much less shot one. Didn't know the first thing about them. But I know a little about this one now.

Four. This is more in the philosophy area than an actual step. There's a difference between getting-by money and getting-over money. If you're willing to get by on a few hundred a week, if you don't have big bills or aren't living large, if you can get by boosting a place once in a while without roughing people up, you might get a scare now and again, but generally you'll be alright. If you've got a thing for authority, though, if you want to show the fat cats, if you want that jar of M&Ms so bad, if you have to have a new Lexus, and if you like to wave a gun and point it at people, eventually they're going to grab you. My message is this: if you want it too bad and think that the money is going to solve all your problems, make you a first-class person, then mister or missus you are preparing yourself for a fall.

Today I went to a new fish taco place, Ruby's, because I keep getting these half-off coupons for their Tuesday lunch special. I'm going to make an appropriation stop there, but it will be a few days. I had the spicy shrimp and bacon tacos.

Five. Do something to yourself that is distracting. I put a mole on my cheek once, a black mascara dot, like Miss Kitty on *Gunsmoke*, and everybody in the store mentioned the mole, but couldn't remember much else about me. I made a special stop at one of the big franchise bagel places and limped. There's nothing people hate worse than to see a woman with a limp. Maybe a woman with a scar on her face. A man, that's different. Says something about character, maybe that he'd been in Vietnam. But for a woman, and the bagel people could only remember the scar and the limp, and that I was very plain. A plain, limping, scarred woman is too much for the average person and they often look away, avoid contact. I got the limp down pretty good. Found a shoe at Goodwill that was built up, so that helped.

And the last thing. Wear a cross. I've tried all kinds of holy paraphernalia. Rosary beads, St. Christopher medals, scapulars, buttons with IHS on them. But the cross is the best. I have a big green jade cross, thick, and on a leather string. Why wear it? God won't be looking down on you if you're robbing, pretty sure. Good luck, simple as that. Wear it on the outside, wear it on the inside. And if it's a Christian place, like Chick-fil-A, they'll definitely remember that.

Whole Foods. This is another place like Walgreens . I like it and there are two sort-of near my house. Run by new-age hippies. And with prices way too high. But I like wandering around the store eating the samples. And when there aren't any samples, like baked tortilla chips, I go and get them off the salad bar. Sunflower Market is the cheap version, but they don't have the samples like Whole Foods.

The scare I mentioned earlier, that you might have one once in a while in this line of work, happened for me at Whole Foods. The armored truck comes three times a week to pick up the big-money deposits. I figured I'd relieve them of some of the burden an hour before they came and I'd have some cash. I was sitting at the lunch tables sipping a chai and wearing my long wig. I'd put my cup in the recycle bin and was headed for the Customer Service desk to make my appropriation. I'd already opened my mouth to say something but hadn't actually uttered anything or opened my purse to show them the Bersa.

And guess who shows? The armored truck with a mullet guard and his gun drawn. He's an hour early and there's a homeless person wandering around his vehicle knocking on the door. The Customer Service man just hands him two big bags of cash and checks—the bags that would have been mine. When the mullet is gone the Customer Service person asks could he help me and I say something about chocolate bars and he points to aisle three.

Wet clean-up at Customer Service, wet clean-up at Customer Service.

Christ almighty, I thought, when I saw that armored car guy with his gun out, how the hell did he know what I was up to? Coincidence, girl, pure coincidence, but the average gun-toting felon would have drawn on the mullet and started shooting.

I had to change how I looked completely the next time, but I made a visit to that same Whole Foods another day. This was one of their smaller stores, and the Customer Service person was different, thank God. These new-age hippies are not so careful with money. At Safeway it's all locked up in a safe and they have cameras and two-way mirrors. At Whole Foods the deposit bags are just down below the counter with the returned items.

Whole Foods shoppers, me being one of them, suffer from the "what's the matter with Kansas" thing. Meaning, go and look at roasted red peppers in the jar. At Safeway they're three bucks. Whole Foods they're four bucks. Exact same red peppers and we pay a dollar more for them—without a squeak. Half the stuff in the store is that way. And Safeway's semi-executive West Coast vice president of whatever is saying in a staff meeting at this very minute what the hell's the deal with this?

But the produce looks nice and they support local farmers, so they say. Which maybe Safeway does too. And they don't speak harshly to their chickens; they just let them wander around—then cut their heads off.

Ralston applied at Whole Foods. He got an interview and they asked him what skills he had, what he was good at. I can't believe he said this, but he told them he was good with money. Yeah, other people's money, not yours, Ralston.

Canon City, that's where he is. Not Supermax, but the old prison on the west end of town. I've been down there twice since he was sentenced. He's sad, and he's gotten a lot older looking, gray skin, yellow teeth. Floss, that's what he said when I asked if he needed anything. After you're in there a little while and they're sure you won't hang yourself, they let you have dental floss. And that has to be a hellacious kind of dental floss anyway to be able to hang yourself with it.

Now that we sold everything but the micro from Engle's house, I have to eat practically all my meals out and wash my clothes at the Laundromat. The bank sends somebody around every few weeks to ask where the money is and to warn us they're going to have to foreclose if they don't receive payment immediately. I've told the gal, it's an old gal with a craggy face, I've told her we're just living with Engle, just renting, and that he's been in the hospital in Albuquerque. What's wrong with him? she asks me every time. I know that if a person is handicapped or incapacitated in some way they have to give you extra time or even suspend payments until you're better or can afford to pay. So I said he had a head injury and might be out of commission for a while. *How long a while?* Ms. Craggy Face asked. I said he won't be able to walk the dog for a long time, and he can't even floss his own teeth. Engle never had a dog, but I thought that might sound convincing.

I had a dog once, Ollie, and used to walk him a lot. This

was before I moved in with Engle. I had a house, a little house, and gradually I let things go. I stopped cleaning up after him, even when he got sick. He had bone cancer and it spread pretty fast. Ollie boy. The vet at Petsmart let me pay on time when he had his first surgery. But the surgery didn't help. And they took care of him afterward too.

A bird would be what I'd get next, if I was going to get a pet. They have them at Petsmart. Parakeets, of course, but they have mynahs, finches, and those African gray parrots too.

I made a "stop" at the Petsmart. This was after Ollie died and Ralston was gone. Not the one next to Target. The one on Hampden. I did my normal walk-around routine, gave them a hundred, and figured out what to do with the car. I was tempted to ride a bike and then stash it.

Petsmart is mostly run by teenagers at night. The regular staff goes home at six or seven. So I figured that would be the right time, towards closing on a Thursday. I was wearing my big cross, a sleeveless sweater, light skirt, and gave myself a beauty mark on the side of my nose. But otherwise I looked like a Mennonite.

If there's a line at the checker, which there was that night, I often have to pretend I forgot something and go get it. I did that twice. The checker was this tall kid with piercings in his lip and ear. Why would they do that, piercing, I mean whoever came up with that? Anyway, tall, cocky, messy hair, some kind of awful-looking polyester shirt.

And for some reason, waiting, maybe because of Ollie, I almost started to cry. But I snuffed it up and The Kid, that's what I'll call him, The Kid looks at me and says are you all right.

"Yeah, I'm all right. You got change for a hundred?"

"Oh, I don't know."

I set the hundred on the counter.

"We're not supposed to take anything over a twenty at night. You don't have a twenty?"

I turned away from him and looked in my purse.

"That's it," I said, "that's all I got."

"Well, I'll have to, like, get the night manager."

"Don't you have another register you can get it out of?"

"I could but I'm not supposed to without the code."

"I'm in a hurry. Do you want me to put these things back and come later?"

"No, I got a bag in the second drawer I could change it out of, I guess."

"Please, I'm in a hurry."

I didn't want to talk too much because I didn't want him to be able to identify my voice. Teenagers are actually better at seeing and hearing things, IDing things most times, even if they do look strange.

When he pulled the bag up I could see it was full of big bills, some hundreds, fifties, and lots of twenties. I opened my purse so I could show him the pistol if I had to.

He counted out five twenties and took my hundred.

"I'll need the rest of that," I said. "All of what's in that bag."

"Right, oh, sure, and I should open the other registers and get the cash out of them too?"

I reached for the pistol in my purse so The Kid could see it. I'd never done that before, only showed the gun without taking it out.

When I pointed it at him he just stood there.

"That doesn't look like a real gun."

"It's a real gun and I'll use it if I have to."

Suddenly I got super nervous and didn't know what to do.

"So, like, are you going to shoot me for this bag of money?"

"I'd rather not."

I cocked the gun but had a hard time holding it still.

"Well, I'm going to get in, like, lots of trouble for doing this."

"Please," I said pointing it right at his chest, "don't be a dumb kid."

I needed to leave and knew someone, a customer, another employee, the night manager would appear very soon. And I didn't want to shoot him, The Kid, with the hair and the piercings, or somebody else.

"Okay, all right then. I guess if you need it that bad I'll, like, give it to you."

"All that's in the drawer and the bag," I said. I saw myself for a moment having to make a decision about killing or injuring another person, or even firing the gun.

I told him to lie down and not to try and follow me or watch me.

"Don't worry," he said, "I'm not going anywhere."

No one was around when I walked out the door, or hurried to the car and got in. It was too quiet, the lot was empty, it felt like just before a tornado, and I thought the F.B.I. was going to open up suddenly, like in *Bonnie and Clyde*, and I'd be ripped apart by machine guns.

Ralston, I said when I got going, *Ralston, what the hell am I doing? You never had to use it once.* I started crying and drove the neighborhoods. I changed my clothes in an alley and threw everything in the Dumpster. The money I stashed under the tire in the trunk and tossed the pistol there too.

What to do, what to do, I said with the windows down, still nervous as all hell. I felt like throwing up.

There's a bar not far from my old house that I used to go to sometimes with Ralston. Engle came with us once or twice. It's on Colorado next to the Indian motel. I thought I'd sit there for a minute, have a beer and wait till my nerves cooled down. I probably wasn't going to get to sleep anyway.

This is a place with no windows, a hot grill up front like at the old five and dime counters, plus every kind of beer neon. And all men. This is not a women's bar. I had to squint at first to see people and the gal behind the counter gave me a nod.

"Let's see, Sippy, isn't it?" she said.

"That's right. And yours is Karen?"

We shook hands across the bar like two men. She's older and has a smoker's voice, with her hair moussed up, which she didn't used to have.

"You alright? Need something to drink?" She reaches across and picks a wig hair off the shoulder of my shirt.

"A little nervous that's all. One of those altercations with a store cashier."

"I hate those. And it seems like they see me coming. Wine or beer? I can't remember what you drink."

"How about a glass of beer and something to munch on?"

Karen set the beer and goldfish crackers down on the bar and went off to clear tables. I turned on my stool to watch. While she wiped a table, one of the men put his hand on her backside and she threw the wet rag in his face.

I didn't want to stay at the bar and only took a few swallows of beer. The crackers were too salty and too, I don't know, cheesy. When I rose to pay, I realized all my money was in the deposit bag, none in my purse, including the change for the hundred.

"Can I write you an I.O.U. tonight," I said.

"Sure, hon," she said. "Hope you feel better."

During the night, I woke every few hours thinking cars had stopped out front and were forming a circle around the house. I looked through the blinds each time and there never was anything. In the morning I got the paper off the porch and wondered if there would be someone parked across the street, watching. But no one was there.

In the Regional Roundup section just after the front page, there was a story about cars being vandalized during one of the forest fires, a sexual assault during a dinner party, the record-tying heat in the metro area, and donations to A MOVIE SHOOTINGS FUND the Aurora movie shooting's fund. Plus a very small story about the Petsmart being robbed.

In the story they interviewed the associate, which is what they call people now who are the peons of retail, and he gave the details about how he'd seen me wandering around the store and then when no one was around I approached him. He said I put a hundred-dollar bill on the counter and when he tried to give me change, I pulled out what looked like a toy pistol. This, of course, is The Kid saying these things, with the hair and piercings.

They said the alleged thief made off with an undetermined amount of cash and checks, which is what they say when they don't want to say. The associate, a boy named Donner, like the reindeer, said I was dressed very plainly, had a skin blemish on my nose, and was wearing clothing to disguise a large backside. I could hear the police and the newspaper people laughing about that one.

Why did he have to say that, tell the whole world?

The Kid.

I was going to get the deposit bag out of the car after retrieving the newspaper, but first I went into the bedroom to look in the dresser mirror. I'd always had a kind of boy's butt, a keister my father used to say, and as a girl I was very sensitive about it. This was before girls could have butts and tell people it was from playing soccer.

But I've been eating nothing but bagels and franchise food for breakfast and lunch and ramen for dinner, cereal at night watching the little TV that we kept, and that kind of food can pack it on. Plus, I hadn't been walking or doing any kind of exercise lately.

The rest of the day I looked in store windows and turned the rearview mirror in the car to see if my face had gotten fat too.

When I counted the money this time I was paranoid and made sure the doors were locked and nobody was around. Somebody probably forgot to make a deposit the day before because there was more than $5,000 in the bag, not counting the checks. That meant I didn't have to make any stops for at least four months, assuming they didn't recognize my big rear end and arrest me.

But here's the thing. The Kid saying that kind of spun me around, got me upset, made me think about high school and the teasing. My shorts, my swimsuit, my skirts, they all looked tighter when I tried them on. Maybe even my ankles, like Froda's, were bigger and my shoes definitely seemed snugger.

Then I started driving around the building, the Petsmart, stopping at the far end of the lot to watch. And each time I did I asked myself what the hell I was doing. I circled the store maybe six times, late at night, and I think I knew which car was The Kid's. I wanted to make sure no police were there or private security.

And for whatever reason, I stuck a new little Bersa in my bag so if I had a problem. What problem would that be, I asked myself? The Kid's not going to be packing. If the police show up, a little eight-round clip isn't going to be much help.

And what will I do once I'm there, what will I say. Look Kid, you never should have said that about my butt, especially in the newspaper. That was totally uncalled for, even though I did rob you and scare you by pointing a gun.

When I went into the store a lady was walking out talking with a little dog in a carrier. I didn't see The Kid at first and the night manager was checking someone out. I wandered around looking at the fish until she went to the back.

"Can I help you," The Kid said to me. "We'll be closing

here in a few minutes." He was carrying a bag of crickets for the lizards. I watched him closely to see if his eyes registered who I was.

"Do you have the retractable dog leashes?" I said.

"For a big dog or small?"

"Oh, Ollie is about in the middle I'd say."

He showed me the leashes and I watched him go back to the lizards.

I checked to be sure the night manager was still busy and then went to the check-out stand and waited. The Kid eventually saw me.

"These leashes are so expensive," I said.

"Oh, we used to have a cheaper one. That's the heavy-duty one."

I said I'd take it anyway and then put a hundred-dollar bill down.

He paused for a moment without picking it up and didn't look at me. He wanted to ask if I had anything smaller, I could see that, but something was jamming in his head.

"Maybe I have something smaller," I said.

"That would be good," he said, still without looking up.

I handed him two twenties, he gave me the change, and then he put the leash in a store bag.

"I want to apologize," I said, "for using the gun on you the other day. That was the first time and I never should have done that."

"But you're not going to apologize for robbing the store?" he said.

"That's a whole other issue," I said, "and I can only take care of one thing at a time."

"Somehow I knew you'd be back," The Kid said.

"How did you know?"

"Because of what I said about…"

"Yeah, it was partly that and partly the gun."

"I almost got fired."

"I'm sorry about that. Would it help if I sent your boss a note?"

"You're joking, right? That's a joke?"

I pulled out the pistol and paused a moment, then set it on the counter. The Kid became very alarmed and pushed his back up against the register. I started to say something else, about not having a job at my age and the fear of being without money, but I could see he, Donner Townsend, the associate, The Kid, was terribly confused by the middle-aged woman talking to him.

Without saying anything else I took the bag and walked quickly out to the car. At that distance The Kid was visible standing there with his arms folded, still at the register, when I started the engine.

Before I drove out of the lot, the lights in the Petsmart went off one bank at a time and eventually The Kid and the night manager exited the store together. On the way to their cars, he was telling her an animated story, his hands gesturing and his face moving, and the night manager patted him on the shoulder when they separated.

I parked at the curb and waited for him to pass on the street, to get another look. He had his windows down and the radio up and was oblivious.

When both The Kid and the night manager were gone, I returned to Petsmart, not sure exactly why, but just to make another pass of the store. I sat idling for a time, looking at my image in the rearview mirror, distorting the lines on my face, thinking of the gun on the counter.

I had seen a side of myself that had never come up before and it really got to me. I was prepared to shoot The Kid and it would not have been that hard. If he had resisted or said something or given me any kind of excuse. The moment passed and only a robbery occurred. But another day, another time.

I pointed the car in the direction of Engle's house, but thought I might stop at the bar and have a drink, cover my I.O.U.

Next day I'd go online and find another roommate situation, this time with nuns instead of robbers. And maybe some kind of regular job.

Allison of China

The package had come the previous day from Yang Li-Song's mother, and even before opening it she knew what was inside. In the kitchen she spooned the new tea into a pot and poured boiling water over it. The simply decorated porcelain teapot was the one her mother had given her when she'd begun to menstruate. That day her mother took the entire morning to show her the proper way to make tea—green tea, red tea, oolong tea, and fragrant tea—and told stories about each one. There are things in life, her mother had added, that you should learn to do slowly and with great patience, like making tea, and in the process you will learn much more about yourself.

As a girl, Yang Li-Song had gotten into the habit of rising early with her father. This particular morning, she had woken early, before Roger, because she wanted to spend a few moments thinking about her life and the events to come. She'd been offered a good job with a prestigious Asian-American company in Shanghai and she was going to have to make some decisions.

Two years ago she'd come to America to complete a master's in business administration and in the end had graduated the top student in her class. But Yang Li-Song still remembered that first month and how frightened she was. Staying in and working at the motel run by the Indian couple, the Indian man and his hands, renting an apartment and finding furniture, getting a checking account with very little money, and finding her way by bus and light rail to the campus—they all felt like insurmountable tasks and she'd considered quitting and going home. Despite being fluent in English, she also remembered having to work much harder than the other students who seemed to do everything so effortlessly.

At the end of the first semester she'd met Roger in one of her classes. Six months later they decided to live together. Roger preferred to use her English name, Allison, but sometimes, when he wanted to make a point, he would call her by her Chinese name. She and Roger were nearly the same size, small and slender, both with black hair, and their friends told them they made a good couple. Her sister, Yang Yi-Mei, had teased her and told her to watch out for the foreign devil—then asked about sex. At twenty-seven, Roger was only the second man she'd been intimate with; the first, her father's friend, Mr. Meng Wen Xie, had been an unfortunate relationship that occurred toward the end of her junior year.

Yang Li-Song sometimes thought that if she turned quickly she could catch sight of the young woman she had been. It seemed only a few moments ago that she'd begun college in Beijing; that she was speaking up in cadre meetings; and that she was meeting Mr. Meng at a hotel a short distance from campus. Sad Mr. Meng, he had come to her dorm for help with typing one evening and then insisted they have dinner after. Soon he was seeking her help on a regular basis and occupying whole days. She could never quite remember at which moment she assented to his touch and from his touch to his embrace.

Though she was nervous and still a virgin, on that first night Yang Li-Song could see Mr. Meng had either never been with a woman or it had been quite a long time. He kissed her awkwardly, touched her roughly, and ejaculated prematurely. He was not attractive, not by any standards, and sometimes she had to turn away or close her eyes when they were intimate. As a girl she remembered Mr. Meng's swagger and his gestures and the stories he would tell her father about businesses he was considering starting. Mr. Meng bought meat from slaughterhouses and resold it to the little butcher shops all over Beijing. He was not making much money now, he told her, but by his projections the meat business was poised to take off.

Yang Li-Song didn't know she was pregnant until her aunt asked if she felt all right and remarked that her normally bright eyes looked cloudy. She said she'd been studying hard and sitting in front of the computer and at times had forgotten to eat. Her mother took notice and sent noodles and *jaotze* home with her and promised to visit. Yang Li-Song continued to see Mr. Meng into the third month and then one evening her mother appeared at the dorm and stayed until late. She began coming in the morning and at night and Mr. Meng was forced to stop seeing her. He called the phone in the hallway often and begged her to please find a way, that he loved and needed her. Early one morning her mother came, got Yang Li-Song up, and took her to the clinic in a taxi. She never asked who the father was and Yang Li-Song never shared it with anyone, not even her sister.

In America Yang Li-Song dutifully called her mother once a week and wrote letters in between. She spoke to her sister as often as once a week in Chengdu, where she and her husband lived. It had been more than a month since she'd spoken to her father, but in her mind she could still see him rising early on weekends and joining his retired friends with their caged birds outside the agricultural college. When she was younger Yang Li-Song would help her father get the birds ready and then they would ride together on his bicycle. She liked to listen to the men as they traded and sold their birds and talked about politics and the new China. When Yang Li-Song began attending the same agricultural college and staying in the dorm, she would take her father a thermos of tea in the grassy park outside the campus and they would drink it together and talk. She knew it hurt him when both his daughters moved away—one to Sichuan province and the other to America. Yang Li-Song justified it by saying she would return one day and make her father proud of her.

At the end of the semester, after they both had gotten their M.B.A.s, Yang Li-Song and Roger had visited his family in Wisconsin and they'd spent two nights at a rented cabin. Because of space, all the women and girls had stayed in one big room and the men stayed in another. Roger's sisters liked to walk around in their bras and underpants, which embarrassed Yang Li-Song. The two women had full breasts and large hips and called themselves dairy cows. When Yang Li-Song put on her swimsuit, they watched and marveled at her girlish figure. Over the past two years, Yang Li-Song had felt herself changing in subtle ways: Before coming to America she'd never worn a bathing suit and now owned three. Before coming to America she'd never eaten Mexican food, but now regularly made burritos for Roger and his friends. And until she came to America she had never had coffee—nor had any desire to try it—but now drank lattes with Roger in the morning and evening. Though she'd changed in some ways, inside she didn't think of herself as anything but a Chinese girl who was living in the world.

On that morning two years earlier, she'd just graduated with a degree in economics and she and a friend were preparing to take a trip with Ibrahim Naz. Mr. Naz was from Pakistan and the president of a silk exporting company. He'd been in China for eight years and his wife and young daughters had remained in Islamabad. He'd been a guest speaker in her advanced international finance class and they'd talked afterward. During the week of the Silk Expo in Beijing, he'd asked if she wanted to work at his company's booth and model clothing. A month later he called to see if she would like to tour one of the company's silk farms and factories in Hangzhou. When she hesitated, Mr. Naz assured her she would have her own room and that she would be with a small group.

In the factory in Hangzhou, Yang Li-Song was amazed at how quickly clothes were cut from patterns and sewn together. Occasionally, at someone's behest, Mr. Naz would stop and ask questions of the seamstresses, all young women, and they would inevitably become embarrassed. At one of the stops, a young woman spoke to Yang Li-Song and asked where she was from and why they were touring the factory. About herself the young woman said she was nineteen and that her husband also worked in the factory. While they were talking she continued working and in a moment of distraction sewed through one of her fingers and had to be taken away. Yang Li-Song worried about what would become of the girl and if she would lose her job.

Once or twice a month, when Mr. Naz was in Beijing, they would meet for dinner and talk extensively about the silk business. Yang Li-Song could see Mr. Naz needed someone he could talk to, someone he could trust, and someone he could think out loud with, but she often wondered why he'd selected her. If she allowed herself, Yang Li-Song could be overwhelmed by his intelligence and his ability to speak fluent Chinese, English, French, and Urdu. Mr. Naz was always a gentleman during their meetings and soon Yang Li-Song found herself confiding in him like she'd never done with anyone before. Under Mr. Naz's tutelage she quickly learned the difference between 3 momme and 20 momme silk, and could tell whether a piece of material had been machine woven or traditionally woven. When she began responding to Mr. Naz with harder questions, he smiled and in Chinese said she was learning.

Mr. Ibrahim Naz wore only the most beautiful silk himself—suits, shirts, socks, ties—and he began bringing her the most exquisite silk gifts. Hand-woven, minutely embroidered, hand-dyed, the material felt like elegant water in her hands. Her roommates always waited up just to see what she would bring back from their dinners. When she brought home a silk matador's vest with brocade, they took turns trying it on. When Yang Li-Song modeled a layered see-through skirt, they couldn't resist touching it. The mysterious Mr. Naz became the source of endless late-night discussions and even some teasing.

The day Yang Li-Song told Mr. Naz that she'd been accepted to graduate school in America he congratulated her, but she could see he was disappointed. The next day he called and offered her a job in his company at a high salary and asked her to think it over. After considering his offer, it occurred to Yang Li-Song that in addition to companionship, Mr. Naz might have been grooming her for a significant position in his business.

As a graduation present, Mr. Naz asked Yang Li-Song if she and a friend wanted to take a trip through South China and end up in Hangzhou at the International Silk Show in May. Initially she'd thanked him and said no but her roommates urged her to reconsider and she called him back. On the first leg of the trip, she and her friend flew to Hong Kong and the three of them took a ferry to Macao. In Macao they visited Portuguese and Chinese bookstores, small Buddhist temples on side streets, and threw dice in the casinos. Yang Li-Song thought South China was very different than the north. They spoke Cantonese, not Mandarin, and she often couldn't understand what people were saying. Eating was much more important, and the food was so much better, and South China was a lot greener and wetter.

Before boarding the train at the crowded Guangzhou railway station north of Macao, they visited an aquaculture field in a narrow launch and ate steamed crab on the banks of a canal. In Fuzhou they got off the train and stayed in a small hotel owned by Mr. Naz's friends, an Australian couple. In the evening the five of them sat on the beach next to a bonfire and talked until very late. The Australians were curious about Yang Li-Song and the graduate program she'd been accepted to in America. She explained it was a master's program in Colorado that specialized in Asian trade and she'd been given a scholarship. They also seemed a bit curious about the relationship between her and Mr. Naz. That night she allowed herself to drink too much wine, something she was unaccustomed to doing, and on their return to the hotel leaned on him in the taxi. She had been watching his hands and face and now could smell him. She swooned at the thought of being this close to a man like Mr. Naz.

At the hotel, in her intoxicated state, she wondered if he might stay and make sure they were safely in bed, but he only helped unlock their door and patted them on the shoulder goodnight. For a moment, she considered calling him and asking if she could stay in his room but fell asleep before actually doing it.

At the silk show in Hangzhou there were manufacturers and vendors from all over the world and at the fashion shows there were models and clothing lines from India, Japan, Italy, Thailand, France and many other countries. To Yang Li-Song's surprise, Mr. Naz was accorded the respect normally reserved for dignitaries and at every event he was seated in the first row. Because he was so busy he asked one of his employees, Hao Wei, to escort the two girls during the three-day event. Hao

Wei was an apprentice designer and liked to be called Rocky. He wore brightly colored bow ties and two-tone shoes and was the first gay person she'd known personally. He spoke broken English and told them that Mr. Naz was the very greatest, number one, and everyone thought he was a genius. Even his competitors sought out his advice and he almost always gave it. Rocky said that during a countrywide competition, Mr. Naz had selected his design drawings from among hundreds of others and offered him an apprenticeship.

At the closing banquet for the show, Mr. Naz and Yang Li-Song sat next to each other and before he got up to give the keynote address, she smoothed his suit and straightened his tie. More than at any other time she wanted to put her arm around him, feel his muscle and bone under her hand, but knew it would embarrass him if she did. As Mr. Naz spoke, Yang Li-Song could feel their time quickly collapsing and was aware that in a matter of hours she would be on a plane home. She'd hoped they might have some time together that night, but the evening was filled with one activity after the other.

When Mr. Naz escorted the two women from the banquet hall at the close of the evening, Yang Li-Song asked her friend to go ahead and that she would catch up. Yang Li-Song led Mr. Naz to the bar and presented him with a gift she'd had specially made. It was a silk shirt of white crepe with beautiful stitching in the collar and down the front. When Mr. Naz thanked her politely and kissed her cheek, she fell against him and began to sob. She reached for his hand and asked if that night they couldn't be together, sleep together, and hoped he wasn't offended by her request.

He wasn't offended, more flattered, he responded, but wondered if he hadn't done something to make her reject his offer of employment. He had given it quite a bit of thought, he said, and one day he could see her running his company.

"Please, please forgive me," Yang Li-Song said, referring to graduate school, "but I must do this. It is something that is very important to me."

Yang Li-Song was surprised when Roger entered the kitchen and put his hand under her T-shirt. He kissed her neck and she could smell his morning breath. With his free hand he lifted her cup and drank the remaining tea. Yang Li-Song resented the intrusive intimacy. Roger asked what she'd been thinking about and she in a flat voice told him "China."

"Are you homesick?" he said.

"Yes," she said, "a little." Roger asked how she felt about them taking a trip to Beijing, that he'd found inexpensive tickets on the Internet. The idea surprised her and she told him she'd have to think about it.

Roger said he wanted to meet her parents, see some of China, and maybe even visit her sister in Chengdu. Yang Li-Song said that meeting one's parents and family had a great deal more significance in China than it did in the United States.

"Yes," Roger said, "and that's something else we should talk about, our significance to each other."

Yang Li-Song was glad when Roger was distracted by her offer to fix breakfast. She didn't especially want to talk about traveling to China or what their relationship meant. In her dream the previous night she'd seen Mr. Naz's dark face and had a conversation with him. She tried hard to remember what he'd said but could only recall that he was pleased she'd gotten her degree.

After breakfast Roger asked Yang Li-Song if she wanted to make love and though she didn't, she said she did. While he caressed her, kissed her, and spoke tenderly, she could hear her mother' s voice in the courtyard of their house, her sister' s unrestrained laugh, and the shuffle of her father' s feet in his slippers. With Roger's arms around her, she turned to watch the white blossoms of the crab apple in the yard and she could hear the sizzing of the bees and the insistent call of the birds. Had it not been for her mother's firm hand, she thought, none of this would have been possible and she, too, could have become a factory girl.

In the shower Yang Li-Song stood under the hot water for a long time. In a moment of clarity she knew she would have to call the company in Shanghai and decline their offer. She knew she wasn' t going to travel to China with Roger and that he wasn 't going to meet her parents. She saw Wisconsin and Roger's family as a kind of American trap and wondered how she would tell him.

While she toweled off and brushed her hair in the mirror, Yang Li-Song hummed a song her grandmother had taught her and her sister. For a moment she could see Mr. Meng's pocked face leering at her nakedness, could feel his coarse hands between her thighs, and could hear his pleading voice, and it gave her gooseflesh.

Then, quickly, she went through her closet and dressed in the whitest outfit she could find. After Roger had gone out, she turned on the computer and composed an email to Mr. Naz to ask if his offer was still good.

Mrs. Brown and the Madonnas

First the sheet and blanket up to my neck. Next the spread. Then straighten the pillows under my head. Then turn and bring my knees together, feet in slippers like two feathers. The pad and pen are there and I make notes while the list is still fresh: remove canned goods and wipe cabinet shelves, return books to library, rearrange tools in shed, pick up skirts from dry cleaning, leave old shoes at drop-off, drag recycle bin into alley, wash and iron museum blouse.

Then after toilet and washing hands and face, the newspaper quickly and two seven-minute soft-boiled eggs. One slice of wheat toast. Two ounces of apple-cider vinegar. Don't want Mrs. Brown gaining weight.

After breakfast, morning meditational. Mr. Brown's old room. Under the Madonnas and in front of the carving. A full thirty minutes. I'm the Protectress of the Madonnas, the Ladies, and the Virgins. But I enjoy the responsibility, take it very seriously, and they have found refuge here.

I brought them into my home and this room when it was clear they weren't valued. There were others that wanted to join us, but they had to stay. Poor things had been in storage all bundled up, not even on display.

When Mr. Brown came home from the Weather Bureau, I

went to the museum. Thirty-six years. He sat down in his chair. Two days, that was all. I told people at church if he'd known, he'd have stayed at work.

Mrs. Brown, I said to myself that next week, you better find yourself something to do or it's going to be your day. I had retired from Sears six months earlier. One of my church ladies told me, she said the pay wasn't any good but it was nice people.

They would have been grown by then, had we had some, but we never had any children to worry about, or their little ones either. But that's a whole different conversation.

Well, all right then. I might just as well tell that story. Much as I can. I've been looking for a way to speak about it for a few years. That and other things too.

Mr. Brown and I, we had an arrangement. On paper, we were husband and wife, but it was a big house, I can just put it that way. We had a life together, did plenty of things, but it was a big house.

I suppose I loved him, in my way, and he loved me for sure. Tried to take care of him, a solitary man, much as I could.

But there is a little bit more to it.

I had me another man. Yes, I did. And for most of that time.

Stuffy old Sears woman like me?

He was my pretty man, but he had things to do. That's what he always said. And one of them wasn't marrying me. God almighty. I don't know about what other women would have done, how they would've conducted themselves. A different way, I suppose. I can't say about all that. And we're years past it now.

Brown and I were engaged to be married. He was always a good man, big heart, and he had a mind. Had to stay with the Weather all those years.

But Delvy.

He came to church one Sunday, the A.M.E. I'd like to meet you later, he told me. Why didn't I say, Oh you would? When he'd call me on the telephone, good God, I thought I heard him singing. Wherever and whenever.

Sister, what you doing? Got you a good man and you treat him the way you do. Couldn't explain it. Never acted like that before in my life. But I never apologized, no ma'am.

Can you live with it, Mr. Brown, I asked him? I'd go away with Delvy sometimes, even lost a job once. He took a couple days to think about it. It was a sadness, I could see it on him, and had it all the way to the end. He thought he could, he told me. He was thinking things would turn around, that I would change. And maybe I thought that myself.

But once or twice a year, Delvy.

And that went on for more than twenty-four years.

Brown had his room, I had mine. I said in the beginning that was how it had to be.

There was never anything at the house, though. I had that kind of respect for Mr. Brown. But we did go places. Mountains in the summertime, state fair, all the way to Canada once. He liked to drive and I liked to let him.

You might say I had the DelVyrus.

There was more to it than that, of course. On my part, mostly.

I looked down the road all my friends and the church ladies were following. I said girl, what kind of life is that? Trading a little security, a little huff and puff, just to have a man, be with a man, sell off part of yourself. Colored people like to pair up, you know, soon as they can, protection against the storm the Bible says, and in past times they needed it. I didn't want that. Not sure what I did want, looking back. More than what I had or what I thought I might get.

But Delvy.

Gone too now. He went first.

Currently just me and the house. And it's a big house.

At the museum Garry Winograd had a show a few years ago, *Women Are Beautiful*. And I was a docent for that. He found some beautiful ones, too. In his most famous photograph, "Histrionics on the Bench," that's the one where the girls are trying to turn away and hide their faces, there's a Black man on the left-hand side talking to a white woman. I pointed that out every time I led people through the exhibit. And that man resembled Delvy, who looked a little bit like James Baldwin, only prettier. Pretty hands and feet, too.

There was another photographer, Robert Adams, who had his exhibit last year. I had the hardest time with that one. Boring. Just pictures, nothing special. Trees that looked a lot like trees. Prairie houses that looked just like old houses on the prairie. And no Black people. The docent coordinator said something to me on the side. I must have let it slip.

And during tours, I had to give the first of my rules. Headphones and cell phones. Which she didn't like either. She was standing at the back once.

"Ionia," she said to me after, "Ionia, be gentle."

Someone has to tell them, and if their parents or friends won't, then... Take them out, turn them off. My goodness, you can't disconnect yourself for an hour or two to look at beautiful art, not including Robert Adams. And when the music comes spilling out or they talk so loud we know everything about the new carpet or the sister visiting from Oregon with her boyfriend. We get it all. Someone has to tell them. But they don't always like hearing it from a Negro witch.

One of those children called me that. Witch.

Man on the bus a few days ago stood up and called two or three of us the "N" word—niggers. This was the day after the election of our wonderful president. I'd forgotten for a moment and looked around to see who he was talking about. The Black man in the next seat touched his arm and shouted "Where, where? I don't see any. Let me run home and get my .22."

Oh, I had a good one at that.

Today you want to offend somebody you got to do better than just calling out names on a public bus.

I drive a car, but I like the bus. The 11 comes right by the house. Mrs. Brown, why don't you take the car, Mr. Brown used to ask me. Truth is I prefer it; I don't like driving a car. I know how, we have two, but just don't like it.

Mr. Ed Ruscha, which people have the hardest time pronouncing, he's another one like Robert Adams. I use what I call the living room gauge: would I hang that piece of art in my living room? Mr. Ruscha, it seemed to me, was trying to put one over on us.

Bad art of mountains with another man's words on top. THE HOLY CON-MAN BEGAN TO EAT. What is that supposed to mean? It's not that I have to have English ladies and gentlemen out in their fields. That seems a little too, well, how to say it, white for me. But there's got to be more to it than that.

It was while I was docenting a group during Mr. Ed's show that I had to say something about another of my rules: clothing. No droopy pants or hats to the side, no flip-flops or sundresses, no T-shirts that show too much or use swear words. Not everyone should be allowed into an art museum, you know. Especially if you're a young man with his arms all over his girlfriend, who has piercings in her privates. If they can't observe the basic rules of dress then they just shouldn't be allowed, I'm sorry.

I used to like to say it slow—Del…Vy.

He never met Mr. Brown. Never in the same building, far as I know. And when he died, Mr. Brown asked if I needed an escort to the funeral. That's the kind of man he was. Del died of the complications. I had myself checked as soon as I knew. Incidentally, I never spent one night in Mr. Brown's room, but that night he came and stayed with me. I wished it had been different.

My third rule has to do with children. They're just too noisy; they make entirely too much noise. I've had to shush them many times. And parents seem to be encouraging them to run amok at the top of their lungs. God forbid if a child should be asked to observe good manners among adults, even reprimanded. They're not really interested in the art, are they? After all, the museum is just a form of babysitting with parents or grandparents there.

Once, when I was leading a group during a tour of Mr. Motherwell's work, a child stuck his finger in his mouth and touched one of the paintings. It was Mr. Motherwell's "Number 70," and it could have used touching up, if you know what I mean, but that's a different issue.

I had to immediately call security and have that child and his parents escorted out. I didn't hesitate for a moment. And the parents were extremely unhappy. But I stuck by my guns. Turned out he didn't do any real damage.

"Ionia," the docent coordinator said, "Ionia."

But I knew I'd done the right thing.

Mr. Brown, he was the one who taught me about doing the right thing. Always the right thing, he would say after dinner when we talked, always the right thing. Mr. Brown had oatmeal every morning for breakfast, including Sunday. Never any fruit or nuts, never eggs or bacon. I make big cheesy biscuits, Mama's recipe. Everybody loves Mrs. Brown's biscuits when I make them on the weekend. Milk and a little brown sugar on his oatmeal, that was all.

When I came into the room the TV was on, but I knew right away. He looked the same as when he was alive. Only like he was taking a nap.

Always the right thing with Mr. Brown.

A few months ago at the Still Museum a young woman definitely didn't do the right thing. She broke another one of Mrs. Brown's rules: No alcohol. She'd had too much and never should have been allowed in. She accosted a painting, pulled her pants down, and proceeded to urinate. God almighty, child. Pulled her pants down. This is all in public.

And her mother was quoted in the newspaper as saying that alcohol caused her to do it. This is a young woman, 36 years old, who has a job in a tattoo parlor. No, dear, your daughter caused herself to do it; the alcohol might have helped, but she was one hundred percent on her own. Imagine that: in front of people and then going to the bathroom. Why would she even think to do something like that?

Don't exactly know why I was so attached to that man. Had lots of conversations with myself. *Mrs. Brown, whatever prompted you? What you're doing is wrong, control yourself.* Hmmm.

Delvy.

We made one together once. I never said anything to either of them. A girl. She didn't have all her internal parts, though, and didn't live. Neither of them could understand why I was so upset. Crying all the time, depressed, had to call in sick for two weeks. They thought it was woman related. Took me awhile, but eventually I got over it.

I was a Cooper before I was a Brown. My father, Mr. Cooper, sounded a lot like Mr. Brown. Or the other way, I suppose. People sometimes had a hard time telling them apart on the phone.

As a child we lived in Pueblo and Daddy told me he'd worked at every awful job a Black man could have in that town. He used a different word instead of awful. Slaughterhouse, section gang, steel mill. He retired from the mill and had a couple of close calls himself. Said he'd seen plenty of men crushed, maimed, burned up by hot iron. Said they called him The Rope everywhere he went. Why was that, Daddy? He'd laugh and say never mind child, just something men say.

My Daddy had the same kind of hair I do. Straightish, not tight curly. Not quite like white hair; almost, but with a wave. We could go to white barbers and salons if we wanted— if they'd take us. Like church, hair is one of those things that's still pretty divided. Whether they can or not, people say they can't cut Black hair.

For a few years I've been going to a little place by the motel, on Colorado Boulevard. She's all right with my hair and knows how to wash and cut it. But she's getting old and sickly. Imagine touching and fixing people's hair for 60 years or so and having to talk to them about nothing.

He had some hair, Delvy. Big black hair, it was soft to the touch, not hard, and I loved it when he combed it out.

Singing is another one of my rules. No singing or loud humming. A man in the Van Gogh show, he had his own head-phones on. I was leading a group and tapped him, asked him to please keep it down. He just looked at me. I know he was thinking witch, and he kept on.

He stopped at "Wheat Field with Crows," and I led my group in a different direction.

Across the room I could see and hear him at "The Church at Auvers."

I wanted to snap those headphones off his head and throw them away.

At "Self-portrait with Straw Hat," the famous one not the first one, he began tapping his feet too.

I said, *what are you going to do about it, Mrs. Brown?* This might require some action on your part. When I saw security I told them. He was also leaning over the barrier way too close. These paintings are worth millions and millions of dollars. Priceless.

They escorted him out. But not before he could call me a name.

When I was a girl, I thought of Mr. Cooper as someone like John Henry. Hard working, dark, and knew how to fix everything. He shrank though in the last years. Wasn't much bigger than me at the end.

Delvy, he didn't know how to fix anything. Not even himself when he got sick.

Museum was doing inventory not long ago. They called regarding the whereabouts of three of them. They'd had them in storage, collecting dust. "Madonna and Child with a Swallow." The little carving of "Our Lady of Sorrows." And the "Virgin of the Apocalypse."

One at a time, over a period. I put them in the car, liberated you might say. They were suffering, like women have had to do for centuries, maybe since the beginning. Look at their faces. Even now you can see it. Oh, they all seem to be saying, oh, the trouble and pain, trouble and pain.

Why do women suffer so? Are we born to it? Do we bring it on ourselves? We suffer when things are going well and when things are going badly.

Mr. Cooper, my stepfather actually, was there at the beginning, and he was the one who gave me my name, Ionia. He'd been in the military during the war, in Greece, near a sea by that name. Some kind of spying I think it was because he wouldn't say anything about it. The greatest time in his life, he liked to tell me, the greatest, and he couldn't wait to go back.

Mr. Cooper's nickname for me as a child was H, mostly because I wouldn't let anybody touch my hair, not till I went to regular school and then later when it straightened out even more. It was his special name for me. I was the only one he gave a name like that to. Not my brother nor my sister. But I never did like it much.

Last night I fell asleep taking a hot bath. I was reading a magazine and it fell into the water. I got so dreamy that I even left off putting Vaseline on my face before I went to bed. The docent coordinator had called me into her office before I left and I was low on energy from that. She was crying and I thought maybe she was having family troubles again, that man of hers.

She left a sticky note that said she wanted to talk.

"How are you today, Ionia?" she asked, wiping her nose.

I had led a private group through Mr. Xu Beihong's work, the Chinese painter. I talked to them about the big paintings, "The Foolish Old Man" and "Tian Heng," but the one I stopped at and spent the most time on was "La Sieste," done during his time in Paris.

It's a black-and-white ink sketch of a lovely young woman taking a nap. Like the Madonnas, it shows the radiance of a sleeping woman, the beauty and goodness, without the pressures and demands of life and the world.

"I'm very fine," I said. "And how are you, Judith?"

She liked that kind of chitty-chat sort of thing, and we kept on about nothing for a while.

At the end of my duty that day I'd had to say something to a woman. A very big woman. She was not paying attention to where she was going or what she was doing. She bumped me and others with her large breasts and hips.

"Excuse me, please," I said, "excuse me." It was when I put my hand on her arm that she got so upset. I just wanted her to take a moment and gather herself, be aware of her person and her space.

"Do you think you can talk to me, dismiss me like that because I'm bigger?"

That's what people say now, bigger, when they mean fat. She was very fat and she frightened me because I'm much smaller.

Then she started a loud howl, like she was having a heat stroke. Her face got very red, and her skin was extremely white. She flapped her hands like a small child. Security came over and then Judith was suddenly there. They escorted her out of the gallery.

"Ionia," she said when we were finished chit-chatting, "you've been one of the best docents ever and I've always enjoyed working with you."

Judith was just a girl out of college when she first came. The docents had to show her everything. And she didn't catch on that quickly.

"Thank you, Judith. I've enjoyed my time at the museum, especially after Mr. Brown passed and I'd retired."

I waited for her to say something about the big woman who caused all the trouble.

"I wanted to talk a bit about the woman in the gallery today, Mrs. Flanagan, she was very upset. She thought you were being cruel to her about her size. Her husband is an important donor and we want to keep them happy. I'm sure you were just trying to direct traffic in your group and didn't mean any harm. At least I hope that's true. But Ionia, I've talked to the executive director and we're going to give you a furlough. Some time away from the museum, to think about things, come back in a year or so. What would you think about that, how would you feel about that?"

Furlough. An interesting word. I take good care of the museum, take good care of its patrons, take extra good care of its artwork and they talk to me about a furlough. This big woman made trouble with her large self and nobody's supposed to say anything because her husband gives the museum money. Everything to do with money in America, everything to do with money.

"Yes, Judith dear," I said. "I've been missing my naps in the afternoon anyway and looking forward to getting my rest. I like that word furlough. It sounds like soldiers and the military after combat. Something Mr. Brown might say."

Judith hugged me and continued to cry and wipe her nose.

When I got home I called Aleen and she said her salon was on her porch now, no more shop, and that she could take me.

Aleen has special shampoo and conditioner for my hair, to sheen it and help it relax, she did the research. Her shop is definitely not a Black salon, but she takes care of me. I wouldn't let anyone else wash and cut my hair. And she knows just what to say. When Mr. Brown died, I went over there the next day, and we talked for a long time while she worked on my hair. Mr. Water had passed some years before so she knew what I was thinking.

I told her about the furlough and that I was so tired. I fell asleep in the chair.

When I got home that's when I got in the hot bath. And that night, lord, I was all around the world. Saw things and talked to people I knew and didn't know. Aunt Gigi was there. Miss Graham, my third grade teacher, too. They told me how beautiful my hair looked. Judith was there, but didn't ever say anything. Mr. Cooper and Mr. Brown, too, but far away and like they were talking through a culvert pipe. Lots of blurry people walking around.

Judith brought Mr. Jules from Security to the house. They had called but I didn't pick up. May we come in? Judith asked. I was still in my pajamas. They said they were looking for three pieces from the Spanish Colonial and Mexican exhibits.

"And you want my opinion about where they might be?"

Mr. Jules, who is Black, said, "No, Ionia, we have reason to believe they might be here."

"That you might have borrowed them," Judith said softly, "and forgotten to bring them back."

I told them they were welcome to look around, and they did. But when they got to Mr. Brown's room they wondered what was in it.

"Mr. Brown's personal effects. That was his room."

"Would you mind if we took a quick look inside?"

The door was locked, which is the way I always leave it.

"Yes, I would. That room has special meaning to me, and I'd prefer not to open it to strangers."

"Well," Mr. Jules said, "we are not exactly strangers, Ionia, and we were hoping to make it easier on someone if they needed to return certain art work. Make it so we wouldn't have to involve the police."

I opened the front door and let them know their visit was over.

Mr. Jules said, "Ionia, Mrs. Brown, please."

After they had driven away I read the paper and changed my clothes. On my list I'd written "laundry" and knew I needed to walk to the store to get detergent soap. But I had to make a stop first to tell my friends that they were safe, that I'd protected them, that they didn't have to worry about going anywhere.

On the way to the store, I'd went to Walgreens first for my special face soap and vitamins, and then I went on down the street for groceries. Aleen's former shop was on the way, next to the motel, and I paused to look in the empty space. I had my hand cupped on the window when the motel woman said something.

"She has gone to her house," she said. "I helped her move the things."

The motel woman is from India.

"Do you drink tea?" she asked.

"Yes, I usually have a cup in the morning. But I had visitors today and forgot."

"Would you like to have a cup of spiced tea, what we call chai?" she asked.

I told her I'd never had it before but was willing to give it a try.

"It must be so hard to come to another country," I said, "to just pack up and leave home. At least you speak the language."

"We speak another language, too," she said, "Marathi. We are part of the Marathi people of southern India."

"Never heard of it," I said, "but beyond the name I don't know anything about the country either."

"It's the language of Madhuri Dixit."

When my face looked blank she said, "The movie star."

When my face still looked blank she got a DVD and put it in the player. A beautiful woman began dancing and singing with a big cast behind her.

"I am Nisha," she said extending her hand, "and that is Bollywood."

Nisha heated tea and it didn't smell like anything I'd smelled before. Maybe a cross between Thanksgiving and corned beef.

"Come on," she said and held my hand while we danced. We followed the woman on the screen. "It's part of your culture, yes, your family is from Africa?"

"Looks like your people got it, too," I said.

It seemed a little silly, the actors dancing, and us dancing in the office of the motel. But I liked it.

And when I sat down in the chair to drink my tea, it felt so peaceful, so relaxing, maybe I even rested deeply for a moment.

A man came in after I'd woken and he thought I worked there. He asked me to get him some more towels, "the big ones."

"How may I help you?" Nisha quickly said to him and did her head.

"I asked your maid here for some towels. Any chance of getting more towels for the room?"

"This is my friend. She is from the neighborhood. I am the maid."

I finished my tea and waved to Nisha. She asked me to wait, but I went on.

As I walked I could hear the strange music from the DVD inside my mind. I could see the woman—the star, and all the dancers, doing their heads.

When the Colorado Boulevard bus stopped, the driver called out to ask if I was boarding. I must have been standing near the stop. I looked inside to see who was on the bus and realized I was confused. To the driver, I said something about Mr. Brown, that I was looking for Mr. Brown.

He waited without saying anything and the passengers watched me. I stepped back off the bus and stumbled, fell as it pulled away. I tore the flesh on my hands and knees, and for a moment I couldn't get up.

I thought of Judith and Mr. Jules and that they would be back with the police.

Mr. Brown, I cried out, *I don't know what the right thing is anymore.*

They'll be back at my house wanting to get into the meditation room.

Mr. Brown, help me, I'm lost.

They'll return and take the Madonnas away from my protection, away from their true home.

Mr. Brown, Mr. Brown.

Aleen of the HairHaven

All she ever wanted was to do hair and then go home. Aleen never wanted to own the HairHaven. At the shop on Colorado Boulevard, she and Deeda Pangburne did hair for older women, as well as for girls who needed big hair for proms and weddings. Rudy and Desmond did all the special cuts and "style" hair for younger women. Rudy owned the beauty shop, and between the four of them, they did a lot of hair. It was an arrangement Aleen and Deeda liked.

One weekend, Rudy went away with Desmond and didn't come back. When Aleen came in Monday morning, Rudy had left them a note:

Girls—Desi and I are moving to Cheesman Park. This part of town is just a little too... The shop is yours. The equipment, the supplies, everything. And this month's rent has been paid. Take care of all the ladies and babies. Luv, Rudy

Ladies and babies were what Rudy called the older and younger women. Aleen picked up the phone and called Deeda. She came right down and sat in one of the upholstered chairs to study the message. After she said "hmm" twice, she walked to the liquor store and bought a pint of schnapps. Aleen drank a little in her coffee and watched Deeda consume the rest between appointments.

When they closed that evening, Deeda kicked off her shoes and said, "Aleen, I believe Sister Rudy done left us a nest egg." And it was true, he had. That night Deeda talked Aleen into going country dancing with her and they stayed out late and ate breakfast together. For the first time in a long time, the HairHaven didn't open until noon.

During the first eight or nine years after Rudy left, the HairHaven continued to be as busy as it ever was. Aleen and Deeda added two young women to do the style hair, and the two older women continued to handle their familiar customers. Eventually the two young women left and started their own shop and Aleen and Deeda hired a succession of stylists after them.

The day Deeda turned seventy-one, she announced she wasn't going to work as hard anymore and began coming in half-days three days a week. *It was just as well*, Aleen thought, *because there isn't that much big-hair business anyway*. When the last style girl quit, Aleen didn't bother to hire another one and business dropped off even further.

One day after closing up, Boyd, a retired trucker Deeda had been seeing a lot of, stopped by to pick her up. Deeda announced that she and Boyd had decided to move to Palm Springs to live in senior housing, get away from the cold. It was a surprise to Aleen, but the two women hugged and kissed and called each other "sweetie." Then, it seemed the next day, Deeda was gone.

Aleen stood in the dark looking out through the neon HairHaven sign, wondering what she was going to do. She had done hair since she was eighteen and, at seventy-two, didn't know another way to make a living. Her husband, Mr. Water, was dead. They'd never had children, and now her best friend was moving to Palm Springs.

During breakfast at the Solar Inn, Marvelle, the owner, told her to close up the shop and put it in her house, "Cut back on all that overhead."

Aleen thought about it. The next morning, with the help of the motel staff next door, she began moving the things she needed, one at a time, to her enclosed porch. During the weekend, she had a garage sale and sold off the pieces she didn't need. She taped a large sign in the shop window that said the HairHaven was closed, and to call her at home for appointments.

Within a few weeks, many of her regular clients had called and made appointments. Most days, she saw two or three customers, and that was plenty. She knew some of them made appointments just to have somewhere to go and someone to talk with. Aleen wasn't ready to sit on the sofa with the remote control, so she didn't mind fixing their hair.

Before Mr. Water had passed, he'd enclosed the front porch so that it was a comfortable place in summer and winter. Aleen kept the equipment there because she didn't want people inside her house, touching things, prying into her life. In a window on the porch above the mailbox, Aleen placed a simple black and white sign that said "Beauty Shop."

Everyone who came to the house wanted to know how Deeda was doing. She told them, "Fine, Deeda's just fine." She and Deeda talked about once a week on the phone, and she often got postcards from Palm Springs and southern California. Sometimes she showed her customers the cards.

"What was that man's name she went with?" Mrs. Maestas asked.

"Boyd," Aleen said, "still is Boyd."

One day, while she was doing a permanent, a customer noticed how scabby and discolored her hands were and suggested she have them looked at. "Overgrown liver spots," Aleen said, "nothing to worry about."

While the woman sat with her hair pinned, she went on to tell Aleen how her niece had to have some kind of cancer taken off her neck and one of her lymph nodes removed. Aleen wasn't really interested in the story, but the woman chatted on anyway about the niece's skin graft from her buttocks and how the first graft didn't take very well and how they had to do it again and how now she can never wear a bikini and how she had such a cute shape.

The spots on Aleen's hands got bigger and turned dark and irregular, and then she finally made an appointment to see the doctor. The doctor himself was dark, Dr. Moreno. In the exam room, he rubbed the back of Aleen's large hands with his thumbs and asked his assistant to prepare for a biopsy. With a small surgical knife, Dr. Moreno removed a piece of skin from one of the spots and placed it on the glass slide. He told his assistant to make another appointment for Aleen in three days. Aleen's bones had been aching for weeks and she'd been feeling nauseous, flu-like, but she didn't share that with the doctor.

That night, when Aleen called Deeda, Boyd answered the phone. He told her Deeda was out at the Knights of Columbus bingo, and he'd tell her to call when she came in.

"Anything wrong?" Boyd asked.

"No, no," Aleen said, "just wanted to catch up."

For a moment Aleen could see herself and Deeda standing in the doorway of the HairHaven. Deeda was petite and outgoing, and Aleen was tall and reserved. They'd been friends for more than forty years. Aleen missed Deeda.

Three days later, after he'd taken X-rays, the doctor sat with Aleen in a small conference room. He had literature in front of him that explained the different types of skin cancer.

"Normally, when we are doing the biopsy," Dr. Moreno said in his accented English, "it takes a week. When I saw your hands, I had the lab rush the biopsy, because I was very concerned. There are three types of skin cancer, Mrs. Water: basal, squamous, and melanoma. Mrs. Water, you have the most serious form of skin cancer. You have advanced melanoma cancer."

Liver spots, Aleen thought to herself, *they're liver spots. I'll rub them with cream every night and they'll be gone in a week. A real doctor would recognize that. I never should have come to this clinic, with foreign doctors. Skin cancer. I'll go home and take a hot bath—and rub my hands.*

When the doctor finished talking with Aleen, he asked if she had friends or family around. She said no, and he gave her the number of the hospice and suggested she call them.

"I'm very sorry to tell you this, Mrs. Water," Dr. Moreno said, patting Aleen's hands, "but after looking at your X-rays, I must tell you—you are dying, and I'm afraid we cannot help you." Before she left, the doctor wrote out a three-month prescription for pain medication and told her she would need it over the coming days and weeks.

On the drive home, Aleen wept quietly. She had never been much for emotion, not even with her husband when he was alive. She watched people coming and going on the streets and sidewalks and thought about how, for most of her life, she had taken care of others, but never found time for herself. Aleen was familiar with loneliness, but now she was dying, and she heard the drone of her own imminent death in her ears. She wished Deeda were there. Deeda always knew what to do and how to handle things. She wanted to call Deeda, but didn't want to bother her or Boyd.

Aleen parked in front of the HairHaven and sat in the car. The store was located next to the motel owned by Nisha and Rajiv, from India, whom Aleen had befriended. It was still empty with a "For Lease" sign hanging in the window. *Maybe I should just go home and call the hospice,* she thought, *get it over with.* Aleen drove the car down the block to the Solar and went in for coffee.

Marvelle came and sat with Aleen and asked if she was feeling alright. "Hon," Marvelle said, "you don't look so good. You want some soup or something? Let me buy you some soup." Aleen struggled to tell Marvelle what was wrong, but couldn't. She put her hands flat on the table, on either side of her coffee.

"Girl," Marvelle said, shaking her head, "you better get you some cream for them hands."

Aleen smiled and asked Marvelle if she had a gun.

"Sweetheart," Marvelle said, "what's an old gal like you gonna do with a gun?"

Aleen explained that there was a fox in the neighborhood that had been eating some of the cats, and the other night he almost got hers. She wanted to wait up a few nights to see if she could take care of the problem.

"Aleen, you ever use a gun?" Marvelle asked.

Aleen lied and said Mr. Water had shown her all about guns.

"Well," Marvelle said, "I got a little pop-gun twenty-two I'll let you have. But you got to promise me you're not gonna go right over to the First National and make a withdrawal with it."

Marvelle wrapped the gun in a white pastry bag and brought it out to Aleen once she'd finished her coffee. Aleen set the bag next to her on the seat in the car and tried not to look at it. She examined her hands on the steering wheel as she drove and wondered how it was these damned dark spots could cause so much trouble. She wanted to be angry at something or someone but didn't know how.

That night, Aleen brewed a pot of strong coffee, took some of the pain medication, and sat in her chair on the back porch with the gun. She'd never seen a fox around her house, but neighbors had told her they had.

With her cat, Stripes, in her lap, Aleen dozed. She imagined a photo album of her life and began to look through its yellowing pages. Mr. Water in his khaki uniform, home from the war. Short Mr. Water, with his big feet and ever-present grin, standing in front of their house in Alamosa, not far from the first salon where she'd worked. Aleen's mother and two sisters at her wedding, standing arms folded, with serious looks on their faces. Her brother Thomas, visiting them from the seminary in St. Louis, looking at the camera just as seriously. And Aleen, standing in front of the shop next to the motel in south Denver, with a hand covering her mouth, looking very serious.

Aleen got up from the chair and went into the bathroom for more medication. Everything inside her rib cage hurt, and her body ached. She made another pot of coffee and wandered through the house, looking in each of the meticulously arranged rooms. *Shouldn't there be pictures and knick-knacks?* she thought. *Deeda had pictures and knick-knacks everywhere in her house. Where are my pictures and knick-knacks?*

Aleen brought the pills out of the bathroom, took four more, and set them on the kitchen table. She held up her hands and spread her fingers and was surprised to see them glowing brightly. The dark cancerous spots now formed beautiful circles that radiated up her arms and over her body in pulsing waves. She went to the porch for the gun.

When Aleen returned, she took the remainder of the pills and lay down on the sofa in the living room. She thought about covering her glowing hands with rubber dishwashing gloves but didn't feel like getting up to get them. Aleen held up her left hand, pointed the gun at it with her right, and tried to pull the trigger, but nothing happened. She found the safety and released it, then fired at one of the circles. The bullet burned through the back of her hand and exited through her palm. The glowing stopped.

Aleen was pleased and folded her hands together across her stomach. When she closed her eyes she could see Mr. Water, grinning, in his dress uniform. She could hear the rise and fall of the blood in her veins and feel the warm wetness on her hands. In the morning she would try to remember to call the hospice.

Dr. Jo and the Importance of Scent

"Raise your eyes high up and see," the man at the door was saying. "Who has created these things? Not one of them is missing."

Dr. Jo had been expecting the man and his wife. They normally appeared on Saturday around nine and then would take five or ten minutes to explain what the passage meant. That morning she hadn't been listening closely and thought he said "kissing."

"Did you just say not one of them is kissing?"

"No, no," the man said, and the couple had horrified looks on their faces. He read the Bible passage again with urgency and emphasized the word "missing."

They'd been coming on Saturdays ever since Dr. Jo had returned. He was a deputy sheriff, and she did medical billing.

Dr. Jo liked it when they knocked quietly, and she always asked about their children and work. They mistook her curiosity, though, for interest in the Bible tracts they left or their brand of religion. But she never went so far as to invite them in and always kept the screen door between them latched.

"Follow along with me," Bev would say and then she'd read a passage about the benefits of knowing Jesus, or the significance of his name, or his predominant qualities.

Dr. Jo wanted to ask them other questions, but they weren't the kind they would have preferred. They were the kind teachers asked students: why they used the words worship and almighty and lord so often or why they said things that seemed so obvious or childish.

But the real reason Dr. Jo liked it when they came was because they had a peculiar smell. And she'd become especially interested in smells ever since her return from China. It began in Beijing with the boy she called Pepe. He had a smudgy smell that was mixed with the fragrance of fried things, which she'd gotten used to and now missed. At first she tolerated the polluted stench of the big city, the clotted, pervasive, diesel-y smell, and then learned to like it—and the drone of the metropolis as well.

Lloyd's and Bev's fragrance was like some kind of heavy cooking or car oil, which she asked them about in a vague way once and they looked at each other and said they couldn't smell anything.

In fact, smelling had become a major preoccupation for Dr. Jo. Wherever she went she sniffed the people around her, like a dog might, only surreptitiously, and she had notes in a journal about memorable people, like the president of the college and the lady who delivered the mail, and how each of her classes and individual students smelled.

Perfume, perfume, she wrote in one of her entries, *today was all about the girls and their perfume. The odor was like a cross between floral and something saline.* And after she made that note she checked online to see if it was true, that there was urine in perfume and read about the pheromonal qualities of musk oil, extracted from musk ox urine and from other animals like the muskrat and beaver.

Dr. Jo wrote extensively about the smell of urine while she was journaling in China and how ever-present it was. She began to think that maybe the smell was what people thought of when they said some place was a developing country or Third World. And though she didn't share this with anyone, she began to pay more attention to her own urine and write about it, too.

Their tea must be a stronger kind because whenever I drink a pot, I can really smell the leafy, weediness when I go.

At first she would simply breathe the odor in the bathroom, then she began putting her finger in the stream and smelling it; then she began placing a plastic cup between her legs to catch it and swirl it, whiff the odor like a wine taster might do. She thought of what she was doing as research, but research for what she wasn't sure, and she never shared the results with anyone.

Garlic, she wrote while she was in China, *they really like using the stuff here. I can smell it whenever I make a stop. And I've learned to tell one veggie from another, pork from beef.*

Dr. Jo took to eating the sweet rice cakes in Beijing and found they had a marked effect on her urine, a saccharine odor, and on her weight, too. Back in the States, she made copious notes about how long it took for the smell of asparagus to make it into her urine from the time it was eaten: As few as seventeen minutes once, she recorded.

And one thing led to another as she went from website to website reading about urine and eventually she saw there was a sect of Hinduism that, as part of their rituals, drank their own urine. And on YouTube there was an interview from *60 Minutes* with one of the sect leaders about him drinking his urine and that it was good for his heart.

When she went for her regular hair appointment, she asked Aleen if she'd ever heard of or knew anything about urine treatments.

"All the Italian ladies around Alamosa, where I grew up, used to use their own urine or their children's on their hair. At my mother's shop she recommended it for dandruff, droopy hair, and even baldness and hair loss. Pretty standard then."

While Aleen moved around Dr. Jo trimming and fixing her hair, Dr. Jo had a chance to look closely at her face. It had a sallow cast to it and Dr. Jo wasn't sure if she smelled like the chemicals in the shop or if she was sick and exuded an odor.

"How have you been feeling?" Dr. Jo asked. Aleen's hands, specifically, looked like she'd been washing dishes a lot because the backs were discolored a light red-blue.

"A little tired," Aleen said, "but it's to be expected."

Dr. Jo wasn't clear whether she meant it was to be expected because of her age, she was seventy-something, or because she was sick.

"I have to sit down a lot more now," Aleen said with a deep breath, "and it's just me at the house. Me and Stripes."

"Why don't you go on home after this," Dr. Jo said. "And maybe you should consider closing altogether, you deserve it. Put all this stuff out in the alley or your garage, be done with it."

Aleen said she'd considered putting the shop equipment on the front porch and seeing a few ladies when they called.

Dr. Jo wondered if she should offer Aleen a ride home just to encourage her to leave.

"How about we go next door and get something to eat," Dr. Jo said pointing with her thumb to the EZ-Life. "My treat."

Aleen shuffled around saying she wasn't sure if she should close up and that her stomach had been upset and regularly had migraines, but finally she consented, saying, *Well, all right then*, and Dr. Jo took her by the arm.

At the EZ-Life, Karen was there telling a joke about the hunchback who was driving to a job interview, and people were already laughing.

"Ladies," Karen called out, interrupting herself, and then continued with the joke.

Hamburgers and onions were on the grill, but the carpet and walls also seemed to exude their cooked aroma and there was a touch of burn in the room from the chili.

While they sat there with their hands folded waiting, a female sparrow landed on the surface of the table next to them. There were bits of food and salt that had been left there and it pecked its way step by step to get them.

Aleen looked around to see where it had come from, as though there might be a flock of them waiting to converge, and then she pointed at the bird and tried to say something. After a moment she cupped her hands around her face to hide the unusual show of emotion.

Dr. Jo put out her finger, as if to lure the bird, but it continued to peck and hop around on the table, ignoring her. She sniffed the room for anything that resembled the feathered creature, but the other odors in the bar overwhelmed everything and though she tried she couldn't detect even the minutest scent of the bird.

Dr. Jo reached out to Aleen and touched her crusty hand. "Is it beyond rubbing them with Vaseline at night?" she said.

Aleen nodded.

Karen shooed the bird away when she approached the table.

"It's not so bad having them in here," she said, "the male's around somewhere too, they got in when we left the doors open once, but they shit all over everything and fly up in people's faces, plus they never order nothing. You gals eating something today?"

Dr. Jo drew in Karen's patchouli oil and she liked the rich tang of it, especially when it was mixed with her smoky, sexual flesh.

"Cheeseburgers for both of us," Dr. Jo said. "And Aleen, do you want a little bowl of chili? Give me a cup of the chili and a big Diet Pepsi to drink."

"No chili for me," Aleen said. "And a Seven-Up because of my stomach."

"You two are traveling light today. Are you sure you don't want a glass of cheap port or a tumbler of Old Crow to go along with your burgers?"

Both shook their heads and smiled back at Karen.

At the bar the owner, Soto, sat drinking a glass of beer and telling a story about when he was driving around the country in his pick-up. He was wearing his Buffalo Bill outfit. Next to him was a blind man, Trevino, who had his dog in a harness at his feet.

The few times Dr. Jo had been in the EZ-Life, Trevino had been there talking with Karen or one of the regulars and occasionally his dog would sit up and, if there was an ambulance passing or fire engine, begin to moan hoarsely and shake its ears. She could smell the dog, a molting lab mix, and once suggested to Trevino that he shampoo and brush him.

"He smells," Dr. Jo told him. "That doesn't bother you?"

"No," he told her, "you smell, he stinks, and it don't bother me."

Dr. Jo considered most of the people at the EZ-Life rude and of questionable character, but she thought of her visits as further lab work, experiments, and research in communicating with another universe. Once when she was alone, she asked Karen how it was talking with mostly men day in and day out. Karen told her she preferred it to women, but that most of them were immature children still working things out with their mothers.

"Do you ever drink beer at home?" Dr. Jo asked Aleen.

Aleen said she and Mr. Water, her husband who'd died years before, used to watch TV on Friday nights and cook popcorn. They'd eat the corn and share two bottles of beer between them, never any more.

"Ever think it smelled like something else?" Dr. Jo asked.

"Something else like what?"

"Oh, I don't know, maybe like someone's pee."

Aleen thought about it for a moment and shook her head.

Dr. Jo breathed in the heavy beer scent of the bar and couldn't help but think of it as the smell of a salty men's room, which she ducked into every chance she got. She wondered if, like perfume, urine was a secret ingredient in some beers.

When Karen came back with their food she said something to her about the odor. Karen snorted the air and shook her head.

"I'm probably too used to it. It just smells like woolly bar to me." Karen sat down with them and asked if Aleen had time to trim her hair in the next few days and she said she did.

"Let me look at those hands, gal," Karen said, pulling Aleen's hands up.

"Probably need a loofa scrub on them with a pure glycerin treatment and rubber gloves overnight."

Dr. Jo nodded her head in agreement and said she told her the same thing.

When they were finished, Aleen insisted on driving herself home even though Dr. Jo tried to dissuade her. While they were eating lunch, Aleen had fallen asleep mid-conversation, one hand poised in the air, just above the table.

Though she had offered her a ride, Dr. Jo was not really interested in becoming all that involved in Aleen's world. She had her own life and responsibilities, her teaching and writing and friends, and didn't want to be roped into Aleen's drama. It was an issue she often debated in her head: How much to give of herself; how close to get to people; when to pull back.

It was the issue she struggled with in China with Pepe, the boy, and what ultimately led to her decision to leave him there, not adopt.

At her women's group, which met monthly at the Perkette, she asked around if anyone had ever heard of urine treatments, and all except one were sickened by the idea of drinking their own urine or rubbing it on some part of their body, or collecting and saving it somehow.

The one exception, Heather, said it was a tradition in her family for the women to bathe and wash their hair in their own urine and she did it as often as once a week. Dr. Jo inadvertently began sniffing her and at one point was sure she detected an acridness.

"That's why there's no gray," Heather said, holding up her hair, "see, something about it keeps the gray away." Heather said she remembered reading that some ancient people in France, she couldn't remember which ones, used to use it to whiten their teeth.

It was also Heather who wondered if Dr. Jo was interested in continuing the discussion over dinner.

In her office on campus, Dr. Jo was sometimes distracted thinking about how women who did it regularly caught the flow and moved it into containers so they could drink it or use it. She wondered if they ever combined it with anything, tea or a smoothie, to make it more palatable, and did they keep it in the refrigerator or out in the garage or in the bathroom? And she wondered what happened when it was that time of month.

Between classes she continued searching for random information about urine on the Internet. She found that birds did not per se urinate, that it was combined into one substance with feces, and that the origin of the phrase "piss like a racehorse" came from when horses were often seen noisily urinating in public, and when they were given a drug to prevent bleeding that was also a diuretic, and, finally, after races when the winners were tested for drugs and horses would be walked until a stream sample could be taken. The urine of cats, she learned, glowed under black light, in Cameroon drinking urine was a crime punishable by imprisonment, during the Civil War the Southern army asked ladies to save their urine to make gunpowder, and urine is 95 percent water, 2.5 percent urea, and 2.5 percent other minerals, salts, and enzymes.

Early in the morning, she learned how to catch her own with very little mess and occasionally drank it. She began to like the smell of it, the briny fragrance mixed with peanut butter or mushrooms or beets or wheat toast or rich coffee from dinner or breakfast. She also noticed that shortly after taking her vitamins, particularly vitamin C, that the stream was a bright yellow.

On the weekends, Dr. Jo began walking to malls and Target and Safeway from her house and cruising them, holding up shirts or soap, and sniffing them roughly. She didn't care when clerks watched, especially at the perfume counter. There was a certain brand of car coat made in Cambodia that had a distinct odor that she couldn't get enough of. It was as if the seamstress had dried herself on it after she'd worked out, or bathed.

In the big department store where it had been hanging on the rack, Dr. Jo was stopped at the door when she left wearing the car coat. She was in a swoon over it but convinced the security guard that it was inadvertent, an oversight, though she hated to give it up. At other stores she squeezed things or rubbed them together to bring out the smell, and at the natural food store she opened jars or containers of sauerkraut, sour cream, buttermilk, and lox.

Toward the end of the semester, Dr. Jo invited one of her male students, a young man from Istanbul, Yusef, into her office when she smelled him in class. He had the combined rancidness of sweat and cigarettes, and he wore the same clothes every day. She found herself wanting to touch him and more than once squeezed his arm and said his name.

In her office, when he stopped by, her hands shook and she had to bury them in her lap. Yusef had a question about an assignment and for a moment she couldn't remember anything that she'd told the students about the exercise. He had an engaging smile, though, and she found his English, though mangled, entertaining. Dr. Jo struggled with whether she should move around the desk and sit in the chair next to him, and when she finally did, and set her hand on his knee, he quickly gathered himself and left the room.

Dr. Jo was embarrassed at first and called after him, Yusef, Yusef, but he was gone. While she sat working at her desk and on the computer, she was remorseful and regretted what had happened. Later, though, when she was home alone, she began to turn the event over in her head, mumbling throughout the house about what a rude boy he was, what a foul odor he had, and how bad his English was. A foreign student in an advanced speech class should have better English, she said, why doesn't he have better English?

During the class meetings from then on, she called on Yusef even though other students had their hands up. When he gave his speech about the Blue Mosque, she interrupted him and was condescending. Afterward, he stood by her office door, but she refused to see him. When the semester was over, she gave him a failing grade and he protested to the dean and then the provost. Both administrators asked her to reverse the grade, but she refused.

As a way of relaxing at the end of her teaching day, Dr. Jo had begun to bathe in her own urine. She used the hottest water she could stand, poured the yellow mixture she'd collected in, and lay there reading a novel until the bath got cold.

Once she'd finished with grades, Dr. Jo decided she wanted to take a trip to Utah, to see the petroglyphs on the canyon walls. She'd been studying the semiology of the figures and was considering writing a book about the artists and what she thought they were trying to say, what they might have been thinking.

The week of the trip, Dr. Jo had all of the clothes she might need laid out on the bed in the guest room. She went through tops and underwear and shoes, swapping things out, holding them up to see if the color was right and it was what she needed. Her clothes smelled like laundry softener, but the room had a musty, closed-upness about it. This prompted her to pull off all the bed clothes and stay up late to wash everything when she caught a whiff of something like old sleeping bag, a smell she associated with men.

After midnight, Dr. Jo crossed through the living room to retrieve what was left in the laundry wearing only her under garments. The lights were off inside the house, but the street lamp showed through the blinds, and she stood in the dark looking out. She wondered what would happen if she went outside and stood in the yard, with hands behind her back or folded in front, like Mary or one of the saints.

She opened the front door and covered herself with her hands, but no cars or pedestrians were on the street. The cement porch was cold on her feet when she stepped out, and she smelled the dusty emissions of the interstate a few blocks away, the oiliness of the refinery north of her, and the body-cavity stench of a small slaughterhouse somewhere near the river. The night was clear and the moon and stars were bright and she appeared luminous. She felt strong and her senses, especially her sense of smell, were alive and she wasn't sure she'd be able to sleep.

From half a block away, she could hear the click-click of heels on the sidewalk and Dr. Jo froze. A short, stocky man with taps on his shoes wearing a small backpack approached and she put one arm up like the Statue of Liberty holding a torch and the other on her hip. The short man looked twice, skipped a click step, then went on without turning his head again. Dr. Jo had the urge to call out to him or get his attention somehow, but instead she went back inside.

That night she didn't change into her pajamas and slept on top of the sheets, under a thin white blanket with the light shining in. She dreamed busily throughout the night of climbing a gravelly trail and woke before seven just as it wrapped around a cliff face.

She tried to call Aleen early that morning because she wanted another haircut, this one very short. The trip was going to be a new beginning, and she hoped to be on the road before nine. In the past she'd planned out her trips meticulously, with gas stops and breaks written on a sheet of paper, and reservations for motels confirmed weeks ahead. She was going to wing it completely this time, and if she couldn't find some place to stay, she'd sleep in the car in a Walmart parking lot with the doors locked.

Dr. Jo wasn't sure where Aleen lived exactly, she didn't even know her last name, which seemed strange after two decades. She'd heard that she moved the equipment to her house, and she'd just have to drive the streets until she found it or gave up and went on her way.

She did remember the cross streets near the house and if she had to, she could go door to door asking neighbors. As it turned out, though, there was one obvious house that had salon equipment in its enclosed porch and a small, painted sign in the window that said "Beauty Shop."

Sitting in her car at the curb, Dr. Jo tried the number she had for the salon, but no one picked up. She got out and leaned against the front fender, smelling what she could of the neighborhood. She had a theory that every neighborhood had its own distinct odor. Some blocks smelled like sugar or dog food or baking or laundry or potting soil or old cars.

When Dr. Jo approached the house, a striped cat jumped into the window on the porch next to the sign and began plaintively meowing. She whispered to the cat and it sang out even louder. The porch door was unlocked when she tried the handle and she called out Aleen's name. No one answered and no one stirred.

The entry door to the main house was ajar and the cat squeezed in then out again as she stood there.

The smell of the previous evening's dinner lingered on the porch and Dr. Jo thought it might have been fish and some kind of cheese. But she also began to distinguish other odors. She was confused by a burned smell, and then something more difficult to detect.

"Aleen, Aleen," Dr. Jo called out repeatedly through the opening in the door, but she was hesitant to enter. She thought if she did it might require something of her, and it might delay her trip. She wanted to help Aleen, though, if she truly needed it, and she wanted to be a friend. Maybe Aleen had fallen and hit her head in the shower. Maybe she'd had a stroke while doing the dishes and couldn't be heard over the running water. Maybe she was still in bed after a sleepless night.

She dialed the shop's number with her cell again, and this time could hear it ringing somewhere in the house.

With her sleeve she pushed the door open and the cat rubbed itself against her legs.

"Oh, god," Dr. Jo said looking inside. "Aleen, what have you done?"

For a few moments she didn't know what to do or who to call.

Without looking back, she retraced her steps and closed the door with the edge of her shirttail. Inside she could hear the kitty's confused call and alarm. And then there was the smell.

Once she was in the car, she told herself, she would try to make sense of what had happened. For a moment she considered stopping at the Solar Inn, talking to Marvelle about the strange, horrible things she'd found, but after circling the restaurant twice, and seeing how fearful she was, she parked on a side street.

But she very much wanted to be on the interstate and out of the city limits. After a time, though, she drove back to Aleen's house, made a call, and waited until someone appeared.

Adelaide and the Special Corsage

A sudden blow: the great wings beating still
Above the staggering girl, her thighs caressed
By the dark webs, her nape caught in his bill,
He holds her helpless breast upon his breast.

—William Butler Yeats, "Leda and the Swan"

1.

She had a four-plex: a one bedroom, a two bedroom, and two studios. Adelaide stayed in the one to maximize the return on her rent, and because she didn't feel she needed more than that. If she watched her budget (she'd paid the place off years before), she could make it through the month on what she took in, with a good amount to spare. And as far as the IRS knew, she only had her apartment and one other.

These were brick apartments, long and narrow, with not much in the way of amenities, except off-street parking in the back. Adelaide kept the yard up with a few flowers here and there, and off to the side was someone's abandoned barbecue grill from years before.

She tended to attract rangy types as tenants; people who

were suspicious and kept to themselves, didn't have pets, and bought everything on sale. She herself was a bit rangy and had a thing for snooping around, asking questions, listening at tenants' doors.

That's how she found out about the bird. She'd been hovering around a man named Philip Perveer's apartment and she thought she heard a low sort of *kar-kar* noise. About then was when Philip, still in his pajamas, opened the door and banged Adelaide, who had her ear close to the door handle, and cut her head.

"What's that noise I'm hearing, Philip?" she demanded, holding her forehead.

Philip gripped the door so Adelaide couldn't see inside.

"What noise? The leaky faucet you promised to fix? That noise? Or the dink-dink-dinking in the pipes? How about the sparking noise when I go to turn on the disposal?"

"You got a bird in there, Philip? You know my rule about pets."

"A bird is not a pet," Philip Perveer said.

"What is it then? It ain't the paperboy."

"I am taking care of a dear friend's companion while she is in the hospital with the gall bladder procedure."

"I don't want a bird around shitting on things, tearing up my curtains."

Philip Perveer was gone early the next morning mainly because his rent was overdue, but partly because he hadn't gotten any money for the bird he'd stolen and wasn't sure what to do with. From the bathroom window, Adelaide watched him pull away and knew he didn't have nearly enough space in his car to haul even his few pitiful things, so she expected some left-behinds.

Adelaide, with short-cropped hair and men's jeans, overalls sometimes, didn't so much mind when tenants left furniture behind because she liked to pick through the good stuff and sell it at her twice-yearly garage sales. And she had plenty of deposit money to cover any problems, including carpet damage. When they left big things, though, mattresses and box springs, headboards, broken couches, that's when she could be heard muttering and cursing as she hauled them out to the alley by herself.

As soon as she finished breakfast, Adelaide got her keys and went into Philip's apartment. It was messy, which was about what she'd expected, and his dirty sheets were still on the bed. There was also a crippled recliner chair and a green, fraying sofa with a sagging lamp at one end, as well as food in the cabinets and fridge. Philip had left his unwashed dishes and pots in the sink too.

"Goddamn your ass," Adelaide said. On the bathroom door she found a note taped from Philip written in green marker.

This one's for you, Adelaide, the note said. *He eats meat and little critters, some fruit and veggies. Name is Tezowsky, like the composer guy. PP*

Adelaide thought at first there might be a pitbull in the bathroom, knowing Philip, and she opened the door very carefully. She didn't see anything right away and pulled the shower curtain back with a snap. She jumped out of the way, in case whatever it was lunged at her, but nothing was there except the nine months of crud Philip had left on the tub and walls.

To the left of the sink, staring out the window at the yard, though, was a good-sized black-and-white bird with a mournful cast to its face.

"Will you look at you," Adelaide said. "I should have known. That son-of-a-bitch didn't want to cart you around and just left you, didn't he?"

She put her hands on her hips and stepped closer.

"Tezowsky," she said to the bird and it pecked at the window and leaned its head against the glass.

She could tell it was some kind of crow, maybe a little bigger, but she'd never seen one that was black and white before.

"Tezowsky," Adelaide said again, and she put her hand out to it. The bird quickly hopped across the sink and the back of the toilet, then preened a moment and looked up at her. A trickle of blood from the cut on her head reached her eyebrow.

"You are a good-looking bird," she said. "Know any songs, Mr. Tezowsky?"

It chattered and made low noises as if trying to clear its throat. Then it sang out its kar-kar-kar like a rooster and Adelaide touched it for the first time with her outstretched hand. She sat down on the edge of the tub and it hopped over next to her. The pied crow shook its body like a dog shaking off water and turned its head as if to inspect her. Adelaide stroked its feathers with two fingers, still a little afraid the bird might flap up in her face and peck her eyes.

She looked at him more closely and thought the combination of black everywhere but on its chest and shoulders made it look like it was wearing a tuxedo with a white shirt. She thought it rakish the way the glossy feathers on its head were combed back.

The beautiful black-and-white bird stepped onto her lap, one leg, gingerly, then the other, and she swallowed hard—from the fear that remained and from another feeling, a deeper feeling. But the bird unabashedly walked to her knee, crossed over, then came back, and stood in the center of her lap, doing what looked and felt like kneading.

When Adelaide had recovered, she quickly brushed the bird away and stood up.

"Tezowsky," she said, adjusting her baggy jeans and thin T-shirt. "I gotta clean this place up, birdie. Get it rented out again."

Adelaide worked at packing up the usable items in the cabinets and refrigerator and tossed everything else. She talked to the bird, kept an eye on him as she worked, and he hopped around and swooped in and out of rooms as she moved from place to place. She wasn't sure what to do with him when she took a load out to the alley, so she tied a string around his leg and attached it to a drawer handle. When she got back, though, he was untied and waiting for her.

"I was hoping Philip would be back by now, birdie, and remember he'd forgotten you. You ain't gonna be living with me, that's for sure. Adelaide's no-pet rule."

After she'd finished, she considered tucking the bird under her arm but then decided to put it in a cardboard box for its safety and hers.

When one of her tenants saw her carrying the box across the yard she inquired what was in it.

"Nothing but leftovers, Lindie, that damn Philip."

"Let me carry it for you," Lindie said.

Adelaide had cleaning supplies in her other arm, but she refused to relinquish the box.

In the kitchen she set it down on the counter and the bird poked its head out when it had sat in the dark long enough.

"We're going to have to find a little someplace for you, birdie. I don't want you pooping behind my drapes and getting into food. And speaking of food, what the hell did that Philip feed you? I didn't see nothing."

At noon Adelaide made herself a grilled cheese with bacon sandwich and the bird came and stood next to her plate while she drank a Pepsi.

"Don't even think about taking none of that," she said. Then she pulled off pieces of cheese and bacon and wheat bread and held them out when she got tired of him eyeing her.

After washing the dishes, Adelaide broke off a piece of chocolate she'd hidden in the meat drawer of the refrigerator and ate it. Then she sat down with a magazine in a comfortable chair. In a few minutes, she became drowsy and the magazine crumpled on her chest and her chained glasses were askew on her face.

While she slept, the bird helped itself to a bag of peanuts she'd put on top of a kitchen cabinet. It pecked a hole in the back side of the bag and pushed the empty shells underneath. Before Adelaide woke, it flew back to the sofa and settled at the top of her right breast. Her breathing grew rapid and before long she woke.

"Oh, you," she said when she saw the bird there. "Like a black-and-white corsage with a beak. We were at the party and he was there. People wanted to know if you were my flower or a bird. And my man friend said it might be the last time, but that's what he always says."

Adelaide wanted to return to the moment and say some-thing to him, ask where he was going, why he couldn't stay, but that was what happened in the dream. And now, with the bird there, for some reason she knew it really was over.

Across the fence, she could see her old neighbor, Adolphus, moving plants in his wheelbarrow. He knew everything about animals and Adelaide thought she would go over and try to talk him into taking the bird, or at the very least tell her what to do with it, and what it ate. Once again, she tied a string to the bird's leg and tied that to the button on her shirt pocket. With the bird on her shoulder, she put on a baseball cap and walked out to the alley and around to Adolphus's work room off the garage.

"What crow?" was the first thing he said when he saw Adelaide and the bird and then laughed and slapped his leg.

"The one my tenant Philip left me, Adolphus. And I got no idea what to do with this damn thing."

"Put a little top hat on him and teach him tricks."

"You know my rule, Adolphus. No pets."

"Yeah, maybe an exception for the landlord."

Adelaide untied the crow and let him hop around.

"And what the sam hill do I feed a bird like this anyway?"

"Baby frogs, crawdads, sparrow eggs, corn, dog food. You see a dead squirrel on the road with its guts squashed out, yank that car over, take your little shovel out and scoop it up. Save it in a baggie for the bird."

"No way am I gonna do any of that for this bird. Are you kidding about the dog food?

"That bird got a name?"

"Philip called him Tezowsky, like the composer. But I don't know how he'd know anything about composers, or birds for that matter, and I don't think he'd had him all that long."

"Dog food will work. And if you practice you can get it to talk, maybe even do some housework."

"Adolphus, don't you need a good-looking pet bird like this one?"

"I'm away too much. But I'm going to help you out, Adelaide. Tell me again, just so I know; you sure you don't want that bird around?"

"He hasn't tried to peck my eyes or cause any ruckus, but I got that rule, and he's a nice birdie and all, you know, but..."

Adelaide looked at the bird softly as it wandered around the work bench, curious, pecking through the jars of nuts and bolts, looking behind things, pulling string.

And then Adolphus opened the back door and quickly shooed it out into the alley, and the black-and-white bird took a few hop-steps on the asphalt and flapped away.

"Adolphus," Adelaide said, surprised. "Adolphus."

She ran out to the alley to see if she could see it.

"That bird is going to find himself some new buddies in a big tree or a good home in no time. And he's probably eating kitty food on a back porch right this second."

*

Adelaide finished what she had left to do in Philip's apartment and then set out for a walk in the neighborhood. When crows flew over she looked closely at their coloring or where they had perched themselves to see if one of them might be black and white.

A flock of colorful, noisy magpies floated overhead and she called out the bird's name repeatedly.

"Tezowsky, Tezowsky," she said nearly in tears.

After she'd circled the neighborhood, she stopped at the coffee shop and took her drink outside to one of the tables. Little birds foraged on the ground for bits of muffin or cookie, and in the trees the robins pealed to each other incessantly. As she was finishing her drink, she thought somewhere in the distance she could hear the pied crow's *kar-kar* and she stood and listened intently.

Walking home she stopped in numerous places and cupped her ear, imagining that she heard the bird coming closer. At the front door of her apartment, she waited to go in, thinking he might present himself and perch on her shoulder in a flurry of feathers, but he never did.

As the evening wore on, Adelaide became resigned to the notion that her bird, Philip's bird, might be gone forever, but every time the house creaked or there was an odd noise, she was at the door or looking out a window.

At night, Adelaide had a special routine she used to prepare for bed. First, she changed into extra-large men's shorts and an enormous T-shirt. Then, she washed her hands twice at the kitchen sink and flossed her teeth. With a washcloth, still at the sink, she wiped her face and body down, including her arms and legs. Then she prepared a cup of double-strength valerian tea to help her sleep. She brought the newspaper into the bedroom, propped three pillows up against the headboard, and began reading what might be called the un-news. She liked the small stories rather than the major headlines and searched the paper back to front to find them. That evening she read about the chimps that attacked and bit the American graduate student at a South African sanctuary. About the man who was collecting a complete set of 660 baseball cards and was only nine cards away from his goal. About the enormous sinkhole in Highway 24 near Red Cliff. About the noisy late-night inner tubers on the Animas River and the sheriff having to come out. About the man who set fire to his wife's wedding dress and skis. About the successful drive-in theater in Fort Collins. And about the footless girl swimmer who would be competing in the Paralympics.

Adelaide could feel herself begin to doze and set the paper down on the nightstand. She finished the tea and turned out the light. When she began the drift from wakefulness to sleep, she thought she heard the bird pecking at the window above her bed. She resisted getting up because she knew it was probably something from a dream.

Sometime during the middle of the night she heard another loud pecking sound and again resisted it. When she had to get up to use the toilet, though, she stood on the bed to look out the window and there she saw the black-and-white corsage huddled on the window ledge.

Adelaide had to open both the window and the screen to let the bird in and said sorry, sorry, repeatedly when she fumbled with the latches and it took a little while. Once Tezowsky was inside, though, he became excited and acted like a puppy, jumping and shivering his feathers and talking excitedly in his bird lingo. The crow seemed to be telling her about where he'd been and his travels and he used his wings to make gestures to emphasize his points.

Adelaide found him terribly amusing and when he hopped onto the footboard of the bed to pace and chatter, she laughed enough to make her eyes tear.

"Oh, Tezzie," she said, giving him a nickname, "I've missed you and was worried you were gone for good. Come up here you damn little dingle bird."

He talked to her a little longer and then Adelaide tucked him under her chin. He snuggled like a kitty and purred in a raspy voice. She fell into a deep sleep and woke only slightly when the bird wiggled its way into her shirt through an arm hole and settled between her breasts with its wings outstretched.

2.

Adelaide was never sure whether to take the bird out of her apartment, because she thought it might fly away as they got into the car, or escape out the window and be struck by oncoming traffic. But he began to make such a fuss whenever she left that she sewed him a hood, like for falcons, and wore a leather patch on her shoulder with a tether.

That day she had intended to go to the HairHaven, to have her hair permed, but when she got there, it was closed. She'd decided to do something different with how it looked; she'd cut out a picture from a magazine, but when she asked at the Indian motel next door, they said Aleen had moved the shop to her house, and they gave her the new address.

Sometimes after her appointment, she would talk Aleen into going next door to the lounge to have a glass of beer and a shot of something. But she was on a mission to get her hair done that day and she wanted to try the new location first.

Adelaide located the house and took Tezzie with her to the front door. She looked forward to telling someone about the bird, and Aleen was always a good listener. She didn't know her that well, but they'd drunk beer and wine together and she'd been going there for more than ten years, even when Aleene's former partner was there, whose name she'd forgotten.

No one came to the door when Adelaide knocked and rang the bell, but the cat crawled up onto a window ledge on the front porch and meowed noisily. The pied crow wiggled out of his hood and threw himself at the cat, and it was so frightened it scampered back through the crack in the inside porch door. Adelaide pushed at the handle after she'd gotten the bird back in place, but it was chained. There was no answer when she called out Aleen's name, and Adelaide finally got back in the car.

At the E-Z Life, Adelaide ordered a beer and a bowl of chili, and Karen, the bartender, asked about the penguin on her shoulder. They gave him half a burger patty on a plate and he used his feet and beak to dismember it. Adelaide explained that the bird had come to her through a dead beat tenant, and she wasn't sure she was going to keep it.

She told Karen about the crow pecking at the window the previous night after Adolphus had let him go, and then him sleeping with her.

"I've had some strange things in bed with me," Karen, the bartender, said, "but never a bird."

Whenever people approached the bar and ordered something to drink or eat, they gravitated to Adelaide and the bird on her shoulder. But when the male customers put out their hands to pet him, he attacked and even drew blood. Karen said that was a lesson she wished she'd learned early in life.

"Now who is this?" an old man said, pointing to the bird but keeping his distance.

"Tezowsky," Adelaide said. "He's a pied crow and he's named after the composer."

"Which composer would that be?" he asked.

"You never heard of Tezowsky?" she said. "He's pretty famous."

The old man shook his head and couldn't figure out who she meant.

Adelaide told Karen that she'd gone to Aleen's house to get her hair done and no one came to the door when she knocked and rang. Oh, she's around, Karen said, but maybe she's out at the store or doing chores downstairs and didn't hear you.

At home, Adelaide sat outside with the bird tethered, trying to decide whether to clip his wings. She held out the primary feathers.

Adolphus was sitting in a metal rocker on his deck and called out to her when he saw the bird. He often sat outside until late in the evening and if Adelaide was in the yard he would call her name and say it in a crude way, especially if he'd been drinking.

"He came back, I see, Adie-got-laid."

"This little son-of-a-biscuit came tapping around at my window a few nights ago about two."

"Maybe he had his fill of pizza from the trash and bad crow stories."

"What do you think about me clipping his wings, Adolphus?"

"That's only if you plan to keep him inside and never let him out."

Adolphus had a big glass of sweet wine in his hand and half of the bottle next to him. He had an open can of tuna and a sleeve of saltine crackers. He asked Adelaide if she wanted to join him.

In her neighbor's yard, Adelaide untied the tether from her shirt and let it drag behind the bird. Adolphus poured her a big glass of the wine and they watched Tezowsky drag the leash and root for insects in the grass.

"You're getting kinda used to that bird, aren't you? I see you taking him everywhere."

"He makes such a racket if I leave him. And he's become so possessive. Almost like a boyfriend."

"Would you mind if I put on some good night music?"

"Go ahead. I'm just going to be here another minute."

While Adolphus was gone, the crow came and pecked at the tuna and broke a cracker up and ate it. He dipped his beak in Adolphus's wine and wiggled the liquid down his throat.

The music started up just as Adolphus returned. He'd set a boombox in the window and it was playing a collection of country-western ballads. Adolphus settled himself, took a big drink, and then half-sang the words to the song that was playing.

"I've seen you walking past the window with that bird in your shirt, Adelaide."

"What, with your big hunting binoculars? That sounds like a first-class invasion of my privacy. This bird has been traumatized and needs all the nice treatment he can get. And I plan on giving it to him."

"You don't let that bird sleep with you do you?"

"Maybe I do, Mr. Nosyface. What of it? It's a big bed."

"Maybe you could use an old man in there with you late at night. Just to keep you warm. Something that black bird can't do."

"It's summertime, Adolphus, in case you didn't notice. I don't need a man to keep me warm."

"You been looking pretty good lately, Adie-got-laid. Don't you want to invite me over for dinner one night?"

Adolphus moved his chair next to Adelaide's and put his arm around her. He leaned his face closer to hers and the bird fluttered up to the back of the chair and climbed on his bicep. The crow's raspy feet and pointy claws made him withdraw his arm and he swatted at it but missed.

"Good night to you, Adolphus," Adelaide said, standing and taking the bird with her. "You have turned into some kind of damn weird person. Or maybe this is the way you always were and I never knew."

"How come I've never seen you with a man, Adelaide? No boyfriends, no husband. You're not afraid of us are you? You don't hate us do you? You don't prefer birds down below to men do you?"

Adelaide was back in her yard, but Adolphus continued to talk to her over the fence and remind her she hadn't finished her wine and that there was still a little tuna and some crackers. She shook her head and the bird shook its head too. Shut your damn trap, Adelaide muttered to herself and her winged friend. Shut it.

Adelaide got the novel she was reading and went to the bedroom to change. The bird stood on the bed and watched.

"What are you looking at?" she said when she was naked and putting her shorts and T-shirt on. "Maybe you're just the same as Adolphus."

In her head she could hear Adolphus's mocking voice, asking why she didn't have any boyfriends or a husband, which more than annoyed her. The fact was she'd never had boyfriends or a husband and at that moment she did prefer birds to men.

"You need to be outside for a while," she said to the bird angrily. "Need to at least be where other birds are. You don't always have to be in here with me."

Adelaide tried to pick up the bird, but at first it scurried away. When she cursed and threw a towel over it, she handled the pied crow roughly and took it to the back door.

"You ain't gonna freeze out here tonight, birdie. I'll come back and get you after I'm done reading. Go visit your friend Adolphus if you get scared and need company."

She tossed the bird into the air outside the back door and it quickly relocated to a corner at the top of the garage. She left the light on and watched for a time until it flew away.

Adelaide struggled to read her book, and after only a page

she put it down and turned out the light. She looked through the back door at the garage, but the bird wasn't there.

"Okay then," she said agitated. "Okay then," and turned out the bedroom light.

When Adelaide got into bed she pulled back the cover and turned over a number of times, drank her tea and took ibuprofen, the combination she used when she knew for sure she wouldn't be able to sleep. When that didn't work, she took off her night clothes and tucked them under the pillow and put one hand behind her head. She fell asleep within moments.

Sometime during the night violent images, wrapped in sheer drapes, overtook her, and they wisped around the bed, frightening her. Adelaide thought she could make out figures, maybe man-bird combinations, but there was an enormous wind, a tornado, and the sound of tapping or ticking—like pebbles on glass. She struggled to wake but couldn't. In the morning when she woke she was twisted in the sheet and incredibly irritated.

After she'd gotten up, with a fierce headache, she stomped her way around the house, still naked, knocking things off tables and bumping lamps. There were dirty glasses on the counter next to the sink and with one hand she swatted them off onto the floor, where some broke. She got the broom out from the side of the refrigerator, intending to clean things up, but instead swept anything that presented itself off its perch: her collection of antique tea cups on a little shelf; the pictures of her nieces and nephews hanging on the wall; salt and pepper shakers on the window sill from all over the world; a framed picture of an important award she'd gotten when she was still working. And while she was in her sweeping fury, she managed to break the glass out of two windows in the kitchen. When she saw what she'd done, she went through each of the rooms in the house and broke out every window with the broom handle.

"No goddamn boyfriend; no goddamn husband," Adelaide said. She was snorting and breathing hard through her mouth, but she wasn't finished and looked around for more places to vent her rage.

She went to the back door and thought if she saw Adolphus she would attack him, but there on the walk was the black-and-white bird with its head tucked in. She opened the door, intending to pick the bird up and cuddle him, but when he didn't move as she approached, she poked at him with the broom. Adelaide's temper roared back when he remained still, and she began striking him over and over in a frenzy with the hard, sewn part of the broom.

When it was over, which it was shortly, when the bird had become completely lifeless, Adelaide fell in the grass and wept in big, swallowing convulsions. No one had seen what she'd done and she lay for a time without moving.

A breeze came through the yard then, sweeping over her body, and the chimes hanging from the soffit clanged out a discordant melody to mark the occasion.

The pied crow remained there for months, and Adelaide watched it mournfully disintegrate, feather by feather, until it was just a smudge on the walk.

The Madhuris of Denver

If you throw a stick in India, Rajiv once told me, the chances are you will hit a Banerjee. And looking back now I think more sticks should have been thrown. But I was a girl of fourteen and he was sixteen and I thought a handsome boy from Bengal state knew something I didn't and would take us places. Mommy told me marry a Marathi boy, she cried through the entire wedding, but I couldn't hear her or my father or any of our relatives.

One thing after another, many of them Rajiv's stubborn mistakes, and before we knew it, we were in Denver. I did not want to come. I said, where is that, Denver? His parents found a motel on the Internet and gave him the money for the down payment, the kind of thing they had done before. What do you know about motels? I asked Rajiv. We will learn, he said. It's America and soon we will have a chain of motels.

When we arrived I was happy to hear that Madhuri Dixit, the very famous Bollywood actress, was living in Denver with her husband, Nene, the surgeon, and their two boys. She was always my favorite, and it was comforting to know that she was there.

It was because of her that I changed my name. In Mumbai we went to the same high school. And then on to university.

She majored in microbiology, and I was business. They called me Madhuri number two then, Madhuri Nisha, and she was Madhuri number one. She was one year ahead of me and there was always confusion, so I changed.

Even in high school she was very beautiful. I liked to think of us as name-cousins, but we were connected in other ways: She was an excellent speaker of Marathi, and I was a good speaker of Marathi. She was an accomplished Kathak dancer, and so was I. She went to Divine Child for high school, as did I. Also, we both attended Mumbai University. Then we both lived in Denver.

And now we're gone. She still has her husband with her, though. But I have left mine in America. For a long time, I liked to think that we had parallel lives, but, of course, it was fantasy. She went on to become THE Madhuri and has returned to Bollywood after being away. I went on to become Nisha Banerjee, of the Bel-Care Motel of Denver, with no children and a Bengali husband with crooked teeth.

Rajiv doesn't know I'd considered leaving him behind permanently; that until boarding today I was going to stay in Mumbai. He thinks I was going to happily rejoin him in four weeks' time after being with my family. I don't want to spend another day at the motel. It is a mess. And I do not want to continue cleaning it up. It makes me shudder just to think of the soiled beds and linen, the dirty carpets, the toilets, the peeling paint. My friends and family would be so surprised. They think we are successful in America, like everyone else.

Rajiv takes money from the motel, he doesn't think I know. He also touches the women who help, and he lies to his family about how successful he is. I could forgive these things, he could change, but he refuses to have himself checked for family reproduction problems, and I have shame when his mother asks what is wrong with me. I didn't tell him, but I went to the clinic and I am fertile. He says that no one in his family has ever had this kind of problem, and it must be mine. Maybe it is just now a vitamin deficiency, I told him, something simple, but he got angry and pushed me away.

It is the place, not so much the people. And Rajiv with his teeth. I like almost everyone who comes around; I enjoy talking with them, especially the women.

The Train

Whenever I talk about America, how it seems like a big locomotive, that so many people are on the tracks in front or racing to jump aboard or trying so hard to hold on, Rajiv likes to say, "You don't want to stop the engine of progress, do you?"

Yes, I say to myself, maybe I do want to stop it, or at least slow it down. We are not all business machines, I tell him, we are not just here to be wage workers, and he ticks his teeth. He likes to think of himself as the minister of finance, and he meets with his friends in the morning to talk about business. It's much worse in India, of course, though Maharashtra, where I am from, is the richest state. But I am observing it very closely here in America. And in India we are at least protected and supported by our families.

Only a few days ago we had the funeral for Aleen, from the HairHeaven, and no one in her family was there. This would never have happened in India. Her old friend from the beauty shop had come and some of the ladies, but in the end she was alone. It was very much upsetting to me.

Over the months I could see she was getting sicker, her eyes and the color of her skin. The cancer. I brought her a pot of red lentil soup, or some other kind, every week, but I don't think she liked the ginger or garam masala. She was good with hair and had been doing it since she was a girl. I let her wash and cut mine. I have easy hair, very straight. And we always talked.

She was like me, though, she did not have any children. And, of course, no grandchildren, or even nieces and nephews. I think maybe she had one once, before Mr. Water. It upset her still at the end, and she never told me, but I think she had to give it away.

Aleen had never been out of Colorado, except to go to New Mexico. She liked to ask about India. She couldn't imagine how we lived, especially when I told her about Mumbai. So big and so many people. She wondered what we ate and if we still carried water. I told her about chaats—vada pav, aloo chat, dabeli, pani puri, that were like appetizers sold by street vendors—and that I very much missed.

I told her about Bollywood and Madhuri Dixit. She had never heard of either and didn't know we watched movies. When she closed the store in the afternoons she would come in and I would put on a film. I had never seen Aleen laugh, but when Madhuri or Aishwarya or one of the others began dancing she was beside herself. I sometimes danced for her myself and showed her modern and traditional Indian styles.

I wanted her to stay at the Bel-Care some nights when she started getting sick, but even if it was late she would gather herself up and drive home. I liked to make a pot of nice tea for us; I wanted to make her feel comfortable. Aleen had a very hard time letting other people help her. And my Bengali husband couldn't be in the same room. He called her a bad Marathi name after she was gone.

When she was so sick I went to her house one morning to pick her up. I thought maybe she would like to go for a drive. We went out to Madhuri's home in Aurora and I told her about being in the same high school and college, how famous she was in my country, and then both of us coming to Denver. This was after Madhuri had already been gone a few months back to India. We parked outside her big house, and I put American music on the radio.

She told me her life was over and that she knew it was only a matter of days. What would you like to do today? I asked. We can do anything you like. She thought about it and wondered if I would hold her, just for a moment. So, we sat together in the car, two women, embracing each other in front of Madhuri's home, and one moment turned into two, and then we drove home.

The Problem

Almost every place along Colorado Boulevard in this area— the bar next door, Walgreens, King Soopers, the bank across the street—they have all been robbed. But the Bel-Care, never. And it is not because we are lucky or Hindus, but we have a secret weapon.

We play Indian music in the lobby and outside the entrance to the office over the speaker. "Dhak Dhak Karne Laga" is my favorite, and I can listen to the whole soundtrack from *Beta* over and over and watch Madhuri. I like to hear "Ek Do Teen," from *Tezaab*, and "Didi Tera Devar Deewana," too, from *Hum Aapke Hain Koun*.

A man came in once with his hand in his coat pocket holding a gun, I could see the outline, and he said, "Turn that raghead shit down, goddamnit." I pretended I couldn't hear or understand him and continued to dance behind the counter to the song.

After standing there a minute he cursed me and then kicked the counter and left.

Karen told me they had been robbed once a week for three months a few years ago. They finally had to hire an off-duty policeman to guard the bar and it stopped. The owner wanted her to carry a gun, but she would not do it.

Karen could be a dancer, though, she likes to dance to the movies with me. Because she's tall and attractive I have given her my saris to wear and she looks like a *rani*. She enjoys it when I am painting the henna on her hands and arms too.

I am thinking sometimes that maybe she is the smart one of all these. I tell her stories of Mumbai and India and she asks very many questions. About the rupee and drinking water, about being a vegetarian, and if I've ever seen a tiger. She especially wanted to know about Rajiv and our first time.

Because Karen is like an older sister, I have told her everything. That it is strictly against our culture to have sex before marriage. And that we waited until our wedding night, even though Rajiv came to my room before. We were like little children, I said, and Rajiv tried to act like he knew, but he did not know very much.

"They're all like that," Karen said, "and trust me, I've been with a few."

I asked about her first time, and she said it was with her cousins, older boys, when she was thirteen, they held her down.

"After that," she said, "all anybody had to do was ask. Sometimes even when they didn't ask. And things haven't changed much."

I was very curious and asked, "Do you have any children?"

"Along the way I got an infection and didn't take care of it. They didn't have any choice but to remove my uterus."

I told her about the clinic, that they said nothing was wrong with me, and to bring my husband back with me next time.

"And our Rajiv wouldn't go?"

"His mother thinks it is my problem, and it makes me very

upset when she asks so many questions and tells me what I should do. All the way from Calcutta she calls and says she lit a candle and said a prayer or is sending tea or that certain days are better than others."

"I am going home," I told Karen that day, "and I am not coming back. Let Rajiv have his own children and take care of the motel by himself."

"Never again to return?" she said.

"Not ever again," I said.

The Return

But, of course, it is not true. I am going back to America, to Denver to be with Rajiv. Even though my family doesn't like him very much they said I must return. They would not let me stay; they said I had a duty to my husband.

I wanted to call Madhuri, ask her advice. What would you do, cousin? Would you go home to your Bengali husband? Would you go back to the motel on Colorado Boulevard? Once I was reading in the newspaper that my friend has the Guinness record for the highest grossing Bollywood film of all time. And every day she is having more and bigger successes. She is never going to go back to America, though, and I will be there alone without her.

Every time when I am in the motel office, I am watching the sidewalk outside and the people who pass, as well as those who stay at the Bel-Care. Some of them remind me of sadhus you will find on the streets of India. The sadhus here have their clothes on, but often they have their heads down mumbling and they are far away, in other worlds, just like the ones in India. Sometimes I offer them food to eat or tea, and more than once a room when there were children, if they were not already guests. Lately, when I have been picturing our Denver motel in dreams, I see it full of American sadhus. Sadhus looking over the railings, sadhus in the office, sadhus wandering the parking lot, sadhus in every room.

But maybe my mission is to take care of these American sadhus. At Divine Child they often asked us about our vocation and our path. I think I will become a bitter person if it is only Rajiv Banerjee and the motel.

In some ways I am glad not to be staying in India. It is so dirty and there are so many people. The paying of bribes is very troubling and even small local people insist. Men still control everything and women, for the most part, are responsible only for the things the men are not interested in. People are too poor and there is no hope. How did these things occur, I asked myself? Not overnight. Moment by moment for a hundred or a thousand years, but it is because we are all agreeing to it.

Like the idea of castes. If people just said no it would be over. In America the caste system is not so strong, and even though there are rich people, they do not strangle the rest.

And something very unusual happened to me when I was leaving Mumbai. After watching Madhuri on TV, I went to her website. I wanted to be happy for her. She was there in the most beautiful gowns and jewelry going to ceremonies and awards, telling us to buy handbags and makeup. I became upset, even ill, and started a letter. *Dear Madhuri. Dear Cousin.* But I didn't know what to say and couldn't finish.

When I return I have decided that I will hire Shelley full-time, if Rajiv will keep his hands away from her. I want to be able to do more than change sheets and vacuum, and she is a good person.

Shelley has told me about growing up in motels and she knows everything about them. I trust her with bookkeeping and housekeeping, something I no longer trust Rajiv with. She has a gentle spirit and works very well with our guests, especially the women. She has found a small place nearby, she told me, but I have not yet seen it. I give her extra money when Rajiv is away, in addition to her wages, because she always does more than I ask.

And I am laughing when I think of her. From someplace, she has gotten a very nice pick-up truck, and she drives it everywhere. Before Shelley I do not think I had ever known a woman who owned a truck, even in Denver, and for certain I had never ridden in one. In India women are forbidden to drive trucks. She has taken me for rides on the prairie east of Denver and it is the most fun. Imagine seeing an Indian woman with sari riding in a green truck.

I have sent Shelley an email about this idea of working, but she has not replied. I also asked her not to say anything to Rajiv when I was returning and wondered if she had time to pick me up in the truck when I arrive.

On the first day back, no matter what Rajiv says, we will make some changes to the motel. We will paint every room; I have already bought some of the colors. Buy new mattresses for every bed. Scrub the bathrooms from top to bottom. And shampoo the carpets. On the second day we will change the sign out front and announce an open house for our neighbors and Indian friends, with a special price for guests.

So, I have decided as long as I'm going to be living there, if I have any say, the Bel-Care will be more than a rundown Indian motel in Denver.

The Fire

The taxi let me off across the street. The driver helped me set my things on the sidewalk. He insisted on taking me the rest of the way to the motel, but I was too devastated. I did not want to get any closer.

Shelley was not at the airport and I felt something was wrong then. I checked my email after landing and nothing. In the taxi the whole way I wondered what the problem might be. I could never have guessed.

Rajiv saw me standing on the other side of Colorado Boulevard and at first did not recognize me. Then when he did he ran through traffic and was almost run over. I could tell; I knew after one moment of looking at him what had happened.

I began to weep and folded my arms when he came close.

"Nisha, Nisha," he said out of breath and put his arms around me. "It is all gone now, destroyed, all the things we have worked for."

He smelled like smoke and there were still police and fire vehicles in the parking lot.

"You will tell me the details of what happened later, Rajiv, but first, was anyone injured?"

"Madam Ada," he said, "she has died."

"Who else, Rajiv? Any of our guests? Shelley, was Shelley injured?"

"Shelley was not here, Nisha, but she is gone."

I stood looking at Rajiv for a moment, his crooked teeth, his foolish, lying face, and then slapped him. At first it was not very hard. But then I slapped him again and it was much harder and he winced and fell back.

"Madam Ada, she was the cause," he said whimpering, "with her candles. Ask the firemen. I told you we should not allow her. But with the insurance…"

"Where is Shelley? Did you bother her, Rajiv, was she running away from you? Do you not think I know about Madam and the Chinese girl?"

"Shelley was killed in the green truck in the mountains. It went off the road and she was thrown out."

I looked at the traffic coming from one direction and then

the other. When I looked back at Rajiv he had his hands over his ears. Never in my life had I screamed. And for a moment I thought I would not be able to stop.

I let Rajiv carry my bags, including the big one with all the gifts, and he put them in the car. Alone I walked around the motel, looking at the remaining windows and hanging doors, at the blackened beds and rugs and nightstands. The wet stench was overpowering.

Room 202 was Madam's room and I stepped under the tape to look inside. Her drapes had melted and the table where she sat with her candles and cards was burned to cinders except for the metal stand. In some of the rooms the paint I had selected, the cans, were there. When I left they were behind the desk in the office.

"The fire definitely began in 202," the inspector said, "but she must have had things in there that were flammable. What was it that individual was doing?"

"She was what you Americans call a fortune teller," I said.

"She had lot of things in there to start a fire, I am thinking," Rajiv said.

He was moving his head like a fool.

"Something in her room acted as an accelerant," the inspector said, "but those cans of paint didn't help either once the fire got started and they exploded."

"We were getting ready to paint the vacant rooms," Rajiv said.

"Had you, um, let's see," the inspector said writing something down, "had you started the actual painting?"

"Shelley, one of our desk clerks, must have put them there to remind the painter when he came."

"Ah," the fire inspector said, "ah, the painter and the desk clerk, neither of whom are here."

The Exit

In the car I did not want to sit in the front with Rajiv, so I sat in the back. This man, I could see his face in the mirror, I had known him since he was a boy.

"What happened, Rajiv? Were you in Madam Ada's room?"

"I stopped to see if things were all right, if she was all right, and if the candles were lit, she had the oil there."

"Rajiv, she had stopped using candles months ago, after I asked."

"I was wanting to please you, Nisha. I hoped the rooms would be painted when you returned."

He glanced in the mirror for a moment, tried to say something with his hands, and then looked away.

How could I continue to be with him? In the same car? In the same room, in the same bed?

I looked at my phone and tried to search for Madhuri's number on her site. What should I do, cousin? Where should I go? You must come home to India, she said, you must come home. I will be waiting for you. Your family will understand.

At a traffic light, when the car had stopped, I opened the back door and stepped out. Rajiv reached for me and horns went off behind us.

It was early evening and I walked until I was tired. Rajiv circled the car and tried to talk me into getting back inside. When he was finally gone I sat on a bench and watched the buses stop and pass on. The passengers looked at me just as I looked at them.

A man pulled up and asked if I needed a ride somewhere.

"I am not from here," I said. "I am from India."

He shook his head and drove away.

I wanted to say to someone, "From a good family and the highest caste. Not an American caste."

But it will be too embarrassing now to go home, to tell my family, to tell Madhuri, what my husband has done to the first of our chain of motels.

About the Author

A. Rooney taught writing at Jindal Global University in Sonipat, India, and now lives in Denver, Colorado. His novel, *The Autobiography of Francis N. Stein: The Last Promethean,* was published in 2019 by Madville Publishing. He has published a collection of stories, *The Colorado Motet* (Ghost Road Press) and a novella, *Fall of the Rock Dove* (Main Street Rag). His stories and poems have appeared in journals, magazines, and websites all over the world.